Mead an
Mead
Three Furies P
Cop

CW01429098

For more information contact
Three Furies Press, LLC
30 N Gould St
Sheridan, WY 82801
(509) 768-2249
ISBN print: 978-1-958099-07-0
First Edition: March 2023

Joshua Robertson

Table of Contents

Joshua Robertson

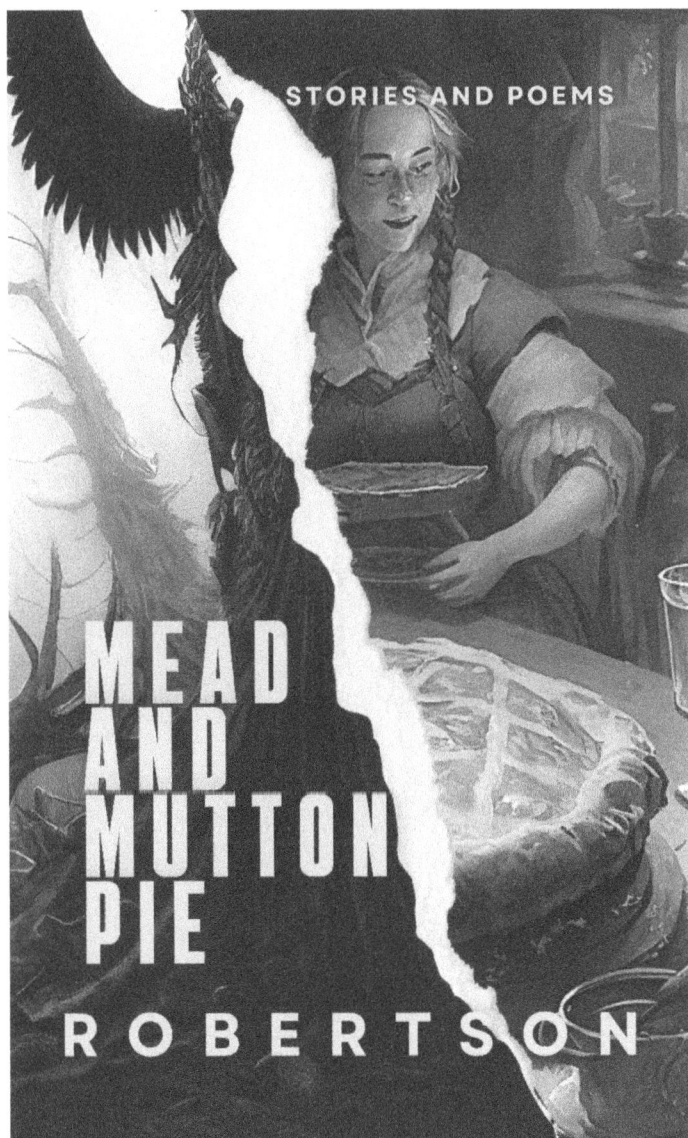

STORIES AND POEMS

MEAD AND MUTTON PIE

ROBERTSON

Joshua Robertson

Grimsdalr

Lo! from the shores of wights, merfolk, and silver,
Sallies the boatman, bearing the Grimsdalr.

The scop stepped clear of the float, joyful that the whale-road was behind them. She turned her attention to the man behind her. The hero who came with her heaved the vessel safely upon the sandy shore and turned it on its end so it would not be swept away by the sea.

No sooner had the bent-necked wood been flipped round, a resident thane drew near them riding his pinto horse. His form, decorated in furs lighter than any she had ever known, vented from the mist that settled against the region.

He halted his horse's gallop and looked down on them, challenging. "Hold, you there, coming o'er the shoals of the waters. Name yourselves. Never have I known far-away dwellers in such small numbers to arrive on this shore, lest they be assassins or spies. Plainly tell me from whence you have come."

She bowed her head, representing herself and her counterpart, and chivalrously replied, "We are from Holmr, sprung from the bloodline of Hraerek, a god among men that only mid-world folk would recall. I am but a scop, a storyteller, Adeline, recording the boastings of the noble warrior-poets of our country. Here, I present such an atheling, renowned on land and sea, Grimsdalr, bairn of Galmr, beloved land-prince of Holmr."

Grimsdalr, a hero in ornamented armor, said nothing, a mountain standing steady in the sand. The carle's light eyes were level with the horse, speaking to the man's great strength. He was a prince among men in his country. His chin was firm, eyes unblinking, standing tall as he waited for his due respect with a hand on the blade hilt against his belt. He was a man deserving of a lesser man's praise. Only noblemen would be adorned as he, with a targe on his back and a brand sheathed on his belt. His mien was striking, even to Adeline, who knew him well.

1

Awe widened the thane's eyes and pulled his shoulders straight. His focus stayed on the hero. "The name Grimsdalr is well-known, even here in the gilded land of Croune. Savants will write about the heroics of the carle titled Grimsdalr for ages. The minstrels will sing about him long through the lives of the children living and the children to come. Your deeds are not held at bay by the watery expanse between us."

Adeline tilted her chin. "Speak your name, thane."

He introduced himself in the formal way. "Crowe hight I, bairn of Johrn, a simple retainer of King Hrackdene, and the warden of the coast."

Adeline dipped her head once more. "We come to speak to King Hrackdene, hearing his cry for reprieve and are glad to have found the land we sought. Is it true that a wight is slaying Croune thanes?"

Her voice was pristine. She did not find joy in the delivery of her message. Instead, Adeline was delighted that Grimsdalr maintained his poise next to her while she spoke as his scop. Like a warrior standing before a legion, Grimsdalr endured his armor without twitching a muscle, speaking to his faith in her, never saying a word.

"Alas," the thane's face fell, his eyes darting to the hero as he spoke, "our kingdom is eclipsed by a monster more terrifying than any known beast, the epitome of resentment and malice. Your heroics are mighty, great Grimsdalr, but a creature as this, you have ne'er contended. Best you abscond from glory and keep your head. I will help you return your vessel to the sea."

He moved to dismount and stopped when Grimsdalr spoke.

"My lifespan would be brimming with long-lasting sorrow if I allowed cowardice to seize my heart. In the coming days, I will be King of Holmr, settling into my father's throne. Hear, no king is truly a king lest he is a war-king. Evil will not 'scape my blade as long as there is a swell in my chest. We did not travel the sail-road for glory to be purloined by a frightened warden." The hero's golden hair, marked with braided strands, swayed against the current along the coast.

The man tightened his jaw but responded with due respect. "Verily, you are worthy, Grimsdalr, but saying and doing are not the same. You know not what the people of Croune know."

Adeline challenged the thane. "You are mistaken. Grimsdalr was destined for greatness since his birthing. On the sharp rocks of the nether, among merfolk and worse, he came into this world at the hand of the boatman." Adeline cooed. "Let him bring peace to your land and save your King from the misfortune that has befallen his subjects. Grimsdalr the Serpent-Slayer will slaughter your monster."

"So be it," the thane nodded. "I will guard your vessel against all injury and care for it well. Stay your feet on the path beyond the hill and you will come to the palace of King Hrackdene."

They said their farewells. Adeline and Grimsdalr journeyed on foot and left the thane on his horse next to the boat. They followed a pathway glistening with pebbles in the midday sun and came by the stronghold in time for their evening meal.

Adeline smirked at the wooden longhouse that was called a palace. It was a shack compared to the stone fortresses found in Holmr. The King of Croune was fortunate that Grimsdalr had come.

A throng of men met them outside the palace. They held wooden spears and battle-boards. A carle with a feathered mantle that veiled his back who stood apart from the rest asked, "From what far-land borders have you come to this cursed place, gilded in such dark-colored furs?"

His liegemen fell in a circle behind the carle of Croune, a testament to the man's greatness and valor, and their safeguard toward him.

This time the scop slowed behind Grimsdalr and bowed her head. Grimsdalr was better suited to address the man who carried himself in equal measure.

"Grimsdalr hight I, bairn of Galmr," he stooped his head halfway. "I wish to be granted an audience with King Hrackdene."

"Mikal'ki hight I, bairn and thane to Hrackdene. It would be an honor, grand Grimsdalr, to present a hero-in-battle. Straightway we will enter to see my father after you have surrendered your armaments."

Grimsdalr did as he was asked, and Adeline had no weapon from which to part. The two traipsed behind Mikal'ki to his father's chambers within the castle.

Passing through the ingress, Adeline was rendered speechless by two heroes who promenaded before her eyes. These carles held the great responsibility to be heroic so their name would be carried through the ages, and it was her onus to tell their story in a way to be remembered.

King Hrackdene sat on his stone seat in an open hall as dim as the grave. He was battle-scarred in his dented armor, sitting on the edge of his seat as though the wight would burst through his palace doors at any moment.

Grimsdalr did not wait for his calling to the court, haughtily uplifting himself with his title. "Hail, King Hrackdene. You know the bloodline of Hraerek, from the mid-world, from which I was born. I am the bairn of Galmr, called Grimsdalr. Sea serpents have I slain, great slick beasts with the strength of a thousand merfolk. The giant-race quivers against the strength of my body. The boatman waits in the nether with mountains of silver from the dead I have sent to his ferry. Even in death, I will retain the glory I seized whilst living. I have come to your kingdom to add title to my name, dear King."

"Welcome and praise, Grimsdalr. I have known your father well, and you are received with equal admiration in these dark days. I wonder what the celebrated Grimsdalr has not achieved from the tales that are told. In war and death and glory, has he known peace or kindness or love?" the King asked.

Grimsdalr said, "O'er the weltering waters from whence I have come, there is no place for such pleasantries. The weird steers men to become carle, and those who are without boasting have not the wits to call themselves carle."

Adeline straightened as King Hrackdene directed attention to his daughter sitting to his side, barely noticed prior. This daughter's splendor was gripping for any man, especially those pulled by an inner hankering.

He waved his arm toward his daughter. "And what of beauty? Does it have no sway over the champion called Grimsdalr?"

Adeline nearly opened her mouth to speak for the hero of heroes, knowing full well that Grimsdalr felt no love or longing for a woman's touch. After days on the whale-road, the carle had not looked at Adeline with more than a passing glance.

Grimsdalr answered him by raising a question to the young lady at her father's side, challenging her notion of glory. "Would you rather die a wife without a name or a champion whose name echoes through the ages?"

The King's daughter sat quietly in the stone palace, stern-faced and quiet until her father dipped his crowned head, giving permission to speak.

She clasped her hands on her gown of fine, blue linen and straightened her spine as if to appear taller. "I am a woman, Grimsdalr, beloved land-prince of Holmr."

Adeline scrunched her face, finding no meaning in the woman's response.

The Grimsdalr remained in posture. Adeline secretly praised him for withstanding such an ignorant statement from the King's daughter.

The woman continued. "My duty is to Croune and is neither the same as my brother's nor yours. The onus is on me to birth the children that will extend our bloodline."

Adeline rephrased, forgetting her place as the scop, holding back her chortle, "You claim that your purpose in this world is to birth bairns?"

"Yes," she agreed. "I will give birth to kings and queens who will shape this country and its citizens for the next hundred years. Without me, there would be none to claim glory and honor like Mikal'ki or Grimsdalr and the men that wage war beside them. Without me, there would be none to boast!"

Grimsdalr's voice filled the space left by the silenced Adeline. "A noble deed, my Lady, and King Hrackdene. But I have no desire to birth heroes to take the glory that I would attain myself. I have not come to Croune to conquer the beast of love, but the beast of nightmares. Forgive me, my Lady."

King Hrackdene's daughter was gentle. "Nothing to forgive, dear Grimsdalr."

"Alas, Grimsdalr, you do not come to unite our kingdoms and speak so fervently. I can only imagine that you wish to battle the horrid hell-monster, which comes from the Blackened Fen, who threatens our beerhall and murders my thanes." King Hrackdene appealed to the carle's vanity. "You must know that this kingdom is fey and to pursue this may leave your father without heir."

Adeline took delight in refuting the claim, finding some strength where the King's daughter had squelched it moments before. "Grimsdalr, even in his younger years, crushed fiends and routed armies—"

Mikal'ki interrupted. "None question the bouts of Grimsdalr, but the creatures fought were capable of being beaten. Our wight is something more; something darker."

King Hrackdene said, "This monster is swifter than a northern wind, in and out of shadowy shapes, and upon you before you take a second breath. It slogs from the Blackened Fen nightly, ascending from the nether, and feasts upon my thanes. The carle, Beow, had his skin flayed and frayed by the beast!"

"Give me control o'er the mead hall this night and I will present to you the head of a monster in the morning!" Grimsdalr declared.

"Verily, you are a battle-bold warrior, Grimsdalr. The boastings of your deeds have merit; alas, we will sing of your courage whether you succeed or nay but first, let us feast and find merriment with wine. You have revived my spirits when no other in my kingdom could."

Adeline was gladdened by King Hrackdene but took a measure of the miffed countenance that Mikal'ki maintained at the pained words of his father.

Nonetheless, the lot went to the mead hall outside the castle and had a blithesome and joyous evening. In a short time, there was loud clatter and laughter among the thanes, athelings, and king. Mead was devoured with duck and danishes and music filled the mead hall.

Evermore night had fallen and the time was late when Grimsdalr beckoned for Adeline to speak on his behalf, as was her skill as a scop.

"The way was set when Grimsdalr boarded the float and mounted the sail-road. He accepted the weird, knowing that he would thrive in his task or die at the hand of the hell-horrid monster. If the last of the Grimsdalr's days are in this mead hall, in the land of Croune, know that it was spent in glee, with honor and glory on the horizon. Sleep tonight in comfort while Grimsdalr, bairn of Galmr, beloved land-prince of Holmr, watches 'gainst the foeman! Bring his targe and his brand; look for a severed head come morning!"

The liegemen and thanes all stood and cheered, hooting and hollering in appreciation of the heir-king from Holmr. Adeline was elated as the people of Croune wished luck upon the hero of heroes and made their exit and returned to their homes.

There were no more words from neither King Hrackdene nor Mikal'ki, and soon Adeline was left alone with Grimsdalr in the mead hall.

Grimsdalr gripped the hilt of his brand firmly in his left hand scanning the horizon through the open doors and waited. Hours passed and finally, he threw the weapon to the side. His targe soon followed, clanging across the floor.

"I will battle this monster with the weapons of nature and nothing more." Grimsdalr gestured to Adeline, removing his dark furs. "Help me remove my armaments. The monster will know what it means to fight a carle from Holmr."

"Your bravery is unmatched, Grimsdalr," Adeline sang, pulling at the knots that held his battle-sark.

The screeching howl that erupted from the fen-moors beyond the palace and the mead hall, from what the King called the Blackened Fen, bespoke of an ancient beast of unholy wrath. The sound was shrill, riding the wind like the deafening cries of battle.

Grimsdalr's clothes fell away and he stood at the ready. "Pull the doors wide open to welcome in the fiend from the nether."

Adeline did as she was told. "For glory."

The shadow of the foeman was barely seen in the pitch of the night. The eyes glimmered, likest to fire, giving credence to the size of the demon. The monster was a giant-type, a master of malice, emerging from the middle-earth regions.

"Adeline, behind me," Grimsdalr stated, stepping closer to the door.

The scop made it to the rear of the mead hall and circled back. The monster was already missing from where it had stood beyond the door.

Nothing stirred.

"Grimsdalr, did it flee?"

Her question was answered as the gruesome wight dashed into the mead hall, as quick as King Hrackdene had warned, and scooped the atheling up in his grasp. Grimsdalr roared and clutched onto the slimed skin of the powerful monster.

The scop was shaken beneath the wisping, black fog that outlined the murky pelt of the wight. Adeline detailed the beast with its enlarged snout and bloodied, ivory tusks that already told of the killing it had done that night. The retelling of this story would clutch at the hearts of the most courageous men.

As the two wrestled, Adeline recalled the boast of Grimsdalr with the warden, Croune atheling, and king. The storyteller knew that he would be determined to fulfill it. Adeline felt her heart flutter as the bairn of Galmr hoisted up and stoutly seized the wight. Grimsdalr's golden hair whipped about the blackened monster, the roars of each echoing in the mead hall. The heir-king truly was from the bloodline of Hraerek, the god of the mid-world folk.

She could only contemplate the silver the boatman would have waiting for Grimsdalr upon sending this hell-fiend screeching back to the nether.

The sound heard was one Adeline never expected. Grimsdalr cried out as his knuckles cracked and the giant broke free. In a flogging swoop, the dire-mooded foeman struck the hero with a felling blow.

Adeline curled back, hiding away from the tormenting scene. The wight's throaty bellow bawled its victory to worlds beyond the living. The scop coiled, feeling powerless against the oversized thing from the Blackened Fen. If death had a smell, it would forever be entombed within her nostrils.

The crunching of bones heightened Adeline's fear. The monster ignored the woman, smashing Grimsdalr's bone-prison, caving in his chest without apology, providing atonement for any death the man had ever delivered. Limb by limb, the carle was swallowed in mouthfuls until all but the heir-king's head was devoured.

Adeline could do nothing but watch the horrid scene.

As the sun rose to the horizon's edge, Adeline discovered that Grimsdalr's foretelling had been fulfilled. The head of a monster was indeed given to the king.

As for the wight, it vanished into the Blackened Fen, forevermore, waiting for another who was plagued with hubris.

Failing Comfort

Sitting on the edge of the bed,
I cannot ignore your weeping,
I fear the tears that you have shed,
How I wish that you were sleeping.

No comfort have I to provide,
Sitting on the edge of the bed,
It would be better had I lied,
Instead of saying what was said.

It was this response I did dread,
A sudden distance between us,
Sitting on the edge of the bed,
The heavy air, thick and unjust.

My fault in thinking as I ought,
Had I known where my actions led,
Look what telling my truth has wrought,
Sitting on the edge of the bed.

Failing Comfort is a quatern that I wrote almost two decades ago after expressing my frustrations in a relationship and then experiencing the consequences of speaking freely. As I have matured, I have learned better communication skills and how to discern the differences between real concerns and those that are delusive in nature.

Joshua Robertson

May Fifth

The fifth of may has haunted me each year,
A day I have feared to shed any tear,
It was on this day my father was born,
Who granted me life, a day I shall mourn.

The child rips out the calendar day,
The man looks back without a word to say,
In youth, his anguish is written in rage,
Torment, etched in sorrow, defiles the sage.

What if my father had suffered his birth?
My life then a shadow, formless and cursed.
Should I end it all? A choice of sheer will.
To save the crying child from tears they spill?

No! While I may forever loathe his name,
By him, I refuse to become the same.

May Fifth was another sonnet that reflected on the emotional connection and rational detachment of the memory of my biological father. Maturing through life and seeking my identity has been a challenge from the time I could ask myself what being a man, a husband, and a father meant. Some days were filled with joy and others with unbearable grief of experience life without a father, and knowing what led to that inevitable reality.

Joshua Robertson

A Princess's Champion

"The savants will write about Pharos for ages. The minstrels will sing about him long through the lives of your children and their children," the heavily armored grunt said gruffly, marching up the mountain pass. His feet fell heavily against the softened soil as he glared at the path before them.

"Pharos was destined for greatness since his birthing, Galmr. He is second-born," the woman to his back said gracefully. With a firm grasp, she lifted her split skirts and dangled her other fingers towards her *Trein-fher*, her guardian. "Galmr?"

The warrior turned and took her hand grudgingly. With ease, he helped the royal princess step over another muddied puddle. "This would go quicker if you would let me carry you."

"I would not hear of it. I am not a saddlebag and you are not a horse," she said matter-of-factly, lifting her hand again.

Galmr sighed and helped her once more.

"Now, what were you blathering on about?"

His eyebrows furrowed at her choice of words but answered. "I was saying that you are also valuable, Princess Emilie. The blood in your veins is the same as any other of the Hraerek family bloodline. Why should you be sent away?"

"Sent away?" Emilie attempted to jump over a puddle, springing forward. The woman slipped and slid, laughing like a child who had just tasted their first cube of sugar. She grasped her hands around her guardian's shoulders, nearly taking him to the ground.

The older man cried out, bracing himself against the light weight of the Princess. He kept them both from dropping to the grime.

Galmr gawked fearfully down the muddied pathway that they had spent the morning climbing. "Stop fooling around! One wrong footing and we are back at the bottom!"

She balanced herself before responding, ignoring him completely. "Father gave his order, and we are to follow. It is not my concern what his intentions are, nor is it yours."

Galmr turned around and grabbed her by the shoulders. His voice bellowed, spit spraying on her cheek. "How can you say that? This is your life!"

"Do not lift your voice at me, *Trein-fher*. My life is not my own. The forthcoming nuptials will unite the northern and western kingdoms, bringing peace while—"

"While Pharos wages war in the east, procuring glory and honor for Florentia," Galmr said with a snicker.

The princess snorted in a manner that was very unbecoming of a lady, especially a noble. She gently redirected the man's hands and reached for her handkerchief, wiping away the droplets of liquid from her face. Slowly, she folded it and stuffed it back into her pocket.

"My blade is hungry for glory, my Princess! You have as much voice as your brother. You could be commanding armies!" Galmr stared at the young girl that he had cared for during the last decade. The woman was the image of her submissive mother and was as ignorant as sheepdip. She had no understanding of men and glory.

Emilie placed her hands upon her hips in the way that women do. "If I am not mistaken, you are jealous of Pharos. Are you implying that you would rather be on a distant battlefield than in my company, Galmr Gurdson?"

Galmr grumbled.

"I can excuse you from your service to the crown. I can rid you of the title of *Trein-fher*, if you wish it."

"I do not wish it, Princess Emilie." The man did his best to hold back a sardonic tone. "I only want to understand why you would rather be a wife to a man that you have never met instead of bringing glory to the Hraerek family name."

Emilie took a moment to look at the stone palace that sat upon the mountain's edge. The castle would soon be her new home with her new husband. She smiled brightly before taking another step toward her fate.

"I am a woman, Galmr," she started.

This was obviously going to be a trying lesson and one that he painstakingly did not want to hear. The *Trein-fher* sulked from behind, keeping his hand from slapping himself in the forehead at his own ignorance. Women would always lecture a man if you gave them a reason. He did his best to listen to the Princess as she attempted to explain her feminine thinking.

"As it was with my mother, and her mother before her, I have been told that my duty to Florentia is not the same as my brother's and neither is yours. The onus is on me and my bloodline to birth the children that will extend our family tree."

"They have instructed you that your only purpose in this world is to birth babies?"

"Yes."

"That is ridiculous!" Galmr cried out.

Emilie turned again, speaking over him as though she were trying to convince herself of what she had been taught, "But I will give birth to kings and queens that will shape this country and its citizens for the next hundred years. Without me, there would be none to claim glory or honor like Pharos and the men beside him. Without me, there would be none to claim anything!"

The *Trein-fher* looked at the fiery princess as she peered down upon him from the mountain pass. The tapestries that hung from the palace walls in the distance could be heard flapping steadily in the wind, but the sound was deafened to Galmr by this untruth. Maybe she held the power of life within her, the fate of men inside her, but she was more than what she was told to be.

Galmr Gurdson the *Trein-fher* moved to the side of the woman, his hand hovering near her shoulder. "You may be the greatest of queens, Princess Emilie, but the only onus you must follow is that of your heart. Forgive me, but what do you truly want?"

Emilie's features softened as she turned to face him. She took a step, so that they stood near the edge together. "That is a question I have never been asked—"

Her voice elevated into a scream as she lost footing. Her skirts flipped over her head along with her feet. "*Trein-fher!*"

Galmr stumbled backward as the woman he loved crashed into him.

Knowing he could not save her, he chose to fall with her. They both flailed over the edge of the mountain to their end and exchanged a kiss they could only share in death.

Joshua Robertson

Once Upon a Time

It starts with *once upon a time*,
When what followed was remembered,
Moral precepts, now engendered,
Verses sullied with gunk and grime,
As stanzas slip from standard rhyme,
And we falter in spoken lines.

Heard around the long-faded fire,
Some words were lost to history,
To narrate myths of mystery,
Inciting anecdotal ire,
To trumpet joy and misery,
Preaching prophesied piggery.

Fated threads, woven miracles,
Of laurels and noted knighthoods,
Of merry men in haunted woods.
Meanings shrouded in parables,
All fouled, misshapen perversion,
Sung and spat as vile aspersions.

Return the mind to tales of yore,
Upon the woes of heroes' end,
The fallen wrest our tears bend,
Where tales are told and hopes are moored,
Yet truths remain, and shall be bade,
The blade may flay, but story's laid.

It ended with ever after,
Vowing pledges of love and laughter,
Let's be certain that we speak true,
Forget the tales we thought we knew,
For not just hope stays our yearning,
The darkness too wants the fire burning.

Once Upon a Time was written in the same pre-romantic style with a clear rhyming pattern as František Ladislav Čelakovský, a Czech poet, who wrote on Slavic folklore and Bohemian songs. I have been such a fan of his work that I included the Frantisek name in my Thrice Nine Legends saga. While I would never claim to be a masterful poet--alas, I am barely a novice--I enjoy the art form as a means of expression and a task to challenge my own creative process.

Ode to the World

O, mundane world, thou art almighty yet,
Clutching mortal men in thy deathly clasp,
Like an artist constructing a vignette,
Thy skilled prowess seizes me in its grasp.

Mine eyes set upon thee, what corruption!
Sloth, greed, lust, envy, gluttony, wrath, pride,
Tendered to plain men, thy execration,
Entice and goad men with all things denied.

A plague has descended upon my heart,
Rendered my soul hapless with somber shame,
Alas, one more dream thou hast torn apart,
Thou providest grief worthy of no name.

O, outlandish world, what dost thou propose?
Or shall we play the wantons with our woes?

Ode to the World was my first Shakespearean sonnet,
published in a collection of American poems by young American authors in the early 2000s. To my knowledge, this has been
out of print and inaccessible for over fifteen years; though, I
have always had an affinity for this set of words. For me, it
speaks to the world tempting men at every turn and questioning how long we can stay on the right path before we lose our
footing or give in altogether.

Joshua Robertson

The Witch and the Old Oak

In a small wooden cabin built near an old oak tree, dwelt a poor young girl with her loving father and mean-spirited stepmother. Her own mother had died when she was very young, and her father had remarried so she would not be absent a woman's influence. They lived in the far north, away from people, where winter always shrouded the sky in darkness and the ground was always layered in frost. And so, the young girl only knew of cold things and suffering no matter the day, yet somehow her heart was untainted by malice.

"Are you fooling around with that *mackare* again, Julia?" her stepmother asked, snorting in disgust.

The warmth of the fire pressed against Julia's rose-colored cheeks as she worked steadfastly on the cloth mask. She meekly replied, looking up at her stepmother, "I hope it will scare away the witch and end the curse of winter and on our house."

"Bah!" She growled in the way Julia imagined all stepmothers did, like a wolf longing for its supper. "I have told you a thousand times over that witches and the like are not real. There is no curse! You should be helping me take care of your father before he is dead like your mother!"

As if on cue, her father coughed harshly from his chair near the fireplace. A quilted blanket was pulled up to his bearded chin. His beady eyes narrowed, the blood draining from his cheeks. "She is not so stupid a child! If I die, please treat her well."

"I will not." Her stepmother huffed. "I will do nothing kind until she grows up and proves herself useful."

"I—" Julia's chin quivered. "I am but eleven."

Her stepmother grumbled again. "I was chopping wood and working the farm at that age. Pa and Ma barely gave me enough time to sleep. I never played." She pointed her finger at Julia's father. "I am afraid you have spoiled this child."

Father shook his head, but a coughing fit took him and swallowed any words he might have said. He hacked until tears swelled, clutching his chest in pain.

Julia lowered her head, turning her gaze from the heated glare of her stepmother, and loosened her hold on the *mackare* in her hands. The mask was soft, much like the feathered quilt in her father's lap.

Her stepmother's scorn tore deep, but she could not believe any mother would be so hateful. It was the witch who had brought the winter. It was the witch who had given her father the sickness. It was the witch who had hardened her stepmother's heart. It had to be!

"We need white-imp mushrooms for the stew, Julia. Run out to the Old Oak and get an apron-full. Be quick about it," her stepmother said.

"But stepmother, why do I always have to fetch them? It is cold out." Julia pouted. "Can we not eat the stew without the mushrooms, just this one night?"

"Do you want your father to die this night, selfish child? Without the medicine in the mushrooms, he surely will."

Her father paused his cough long enough to tilt his head at Julia. "Listen to your stepmother, young lady."

"Hardly a lady," her stepmother mocked.

Julia sniffled.

"Child?" her father strained.

"I will do it, father. Do not worry. I will fetch them at once."

Satisfied, her father sank into his chair once more, and her stepmother returned to stirring the stew. Aside from her father's coughing, the cabin was still in uncomfortable silence while Julia dressed to step into the bite of winter.

She tugged on her long stockings. Made from thick wool, they were itchy but necessary to keep her legs warm. Julia then pulled on her sewn boots, her double-laced sheepskin coat, her threaded hat, and her crocheted mittens. She pulled the cap snuggly over her ears. Lastly, without her father or stepmother's knowing, she shoved the *mackare* into her coat pocket with her fist.

As she exited the cabin, she was reminded to hurry before the late-night chill set. The boarded door thudded behind her against its wooden frame. She set off to the oak tree where the fungus was known to sprout from the whitish-gray bark.

With every step, Julia's feet penetrated knee-deep into the icy wetness that blanketed the world around her. She was sure to take careful steps. She did not want to twist her ankle when pulling her feet from the cold pits of snow.

As always, she checked over her shoulder for her path of footprints that led back toward the cabin. She did not know why but she always expected her footprints to disappear in the snow causing her to become lost in the frozen wasteland of the north. But the snow prints always remained. Sometimes, on her way back home, she played a game to see how quickly she could step back into her old footsteps and race back home to the warm fire inside. But such games always ended with her falling face first into the frost.

With a grin, she decided she would play the game anyway after retrieving the mushrooms, even if her stepmother did complain about her getting her mittens wet.

The Old Oak stood like a sentinel where it always stood. It towered above the world like an omnipotent god, shepherding a flock which may have been created for nothing more than to marvel at its glory. The roots spun like whitecaps around the base of the tree, in and out of the ground, like oversized vines trying to catch a glimpse of the life that they gave nurturance. The Old Oak would be nothing without the roots. If she were a bit older, Julia might have speculated on how she was like the roots and her parents were like the tree; they certainly relied on her to maintain their own livelihood. Why else would she be out here traipsing through the frost looking for stew ingredients?

"Okay, Old Oak, where are you hiding those *white-imp mushrooms?*" Julia raised her eyebrows as she imitated her stepmother's voice. It sounded strange coming off her tongue and she decided that she did not like the tone. Her light eyes gazed around the base of the tree, packed with snow. Somewhere, beneath the haze of white, she would find those precious mushrooms that might keep her father from dying.

Julia sensibly climbed and ducked, scaled, and stooped through the uprooted roots to reach the base of the Old Oak. It was there that she started digging in the snow. She flung white fluff to either side searching for the mushrooms.

"Come on…come on…," she crooned. "Why are they buried so deep? I am trying to hurry, Father. Please do not be angry, Stepmother!"

Julia furiously dug until her little fingers were freezing through her mittens and her stockings were soaked. The snow piled up on either side of her as she pitted herself against the base of the Old Oak. Finally, the top of a white-imp mushroom became visible.

Julia smiled in victory.

She scooted away the snow on either side of the mushroom and found several more growing snuggly next to it. Hastily, she began to pluck the toadstools and fill her front apron.

The earth beneath her feet shifted slightly as her weight pressed against the snow. She did not pay any attention to the small alteration. Julia simply continued her work. She would need an apron-full before her work was complete.

"No!" Julia gasped as the ground suddenly fell away from beneath her feet. The snow and dirt collapsed inward and formed an abyss beneath her toes. Her hands flew into the air as white-imp mushrooms rained down around her. She plummeted into darkness.

The hollowed pitch of the under-earth silenced her screams.

Julia did not know how long she fell, but soon her voice had grown hoarse and she stopped her shrill shrieks. The hole was damp, dreary, and terribly dire. Roots of the Old Oak jutted from the walls, and slimed snakes fell from the sides, most of which Julia did not even see until she was flailing past them.

She found herself lucky that she did not collide with anything and as she neared the bottom of this terrible hole, her body slowed in its descent. A blue crystal at the bottom shined a pastel light, illuminating the area. Julia watched it intensely as her feet landed delicately on the tender soil.

What strange magic had brought her here?

"Hello?" she whispered, not sure whether she should be frightened or amazed at the sight before her. Her eyes shined from the radiance of the crystal that brightened the cavern and the many tunnels that stretched in all directions.

At the sound of her voice, hissing echoed from the tunnels. In a moment's time, slithering snakes of many lengths and colors slinked and slunk into the cavern. Their swarming bodies etched over one another by the hundreds, swirling around poor Julia.

Julia swallowed the scream that crawled up her throat; tears touched the ducts of her eyes. The piercing black eyes of every reptilian monstrosity seemed to be fully locked upon the young girl, hungrily advancing, but not daring to touch her. Instead, the snakes simply circled her, keeping her trapped within the framework of their slimy, boneless frames.

"Hello, dear Julia." A woman appeared behind her.

"Hello," Julia responded back quickly, as a good child would do, before she had a chance to turn around. However, she nearly bit her tongue when she did spin on her heel. Sitting atop the snakes with an evil grin upon her face was the witch!

Julia fought to maintain her composure, refusing to squeak as a scared mouse might do. Even in the presence of the witch with her sunken eyes, inflamed lips, and watery skin, Julia knew that she mustn't be afraid.

"Where am I? Did you bring me here?"

The witch preserved her sinister grin, "Yes, dear Julia. I have brought you to the underworld to give you a gift."

"A gift?"

Julia was confused. In all of her life, she had never been given a gift before. This was really something!

"Yes," the witch said as she rustled, the snakes still entwined beneath her. "I will give you the gift to speak the language of worldly plants and know their powers of medicine and healing!"

Julia widened her eyes at the thought. "I could heal my father from his sickness! My stepmother would love me forever if I could do that!"

The witch nodded, leering down upon the girl from her throne of snakes.

Julia's mind raced over the possibilities before she remembered to whom she spoke. "Hold on a minute! What do I have to do to get this power?"

"Nothing really," the witch said. "I will give you the power in this very moment. All you will have to do is stay with me for nine years, here in the underworld."

"Nine years!" Julia nearly fell back into the snakes. "My father will be dead in nine years! What good is the power if I cannot save my father?"

"Your father will die eventually, dear Julia. Besides, do you really think that you will be missed? I am terribly lonely in the underworld and have always wanted a daughter to love. No one ever visits."

Julia looked about her, jamming her hands into her coat pocket, a gleam flashing across her eye. "That must be really hard for you."

"It is," the witch said in a singsong tone.

"I would like to help you, but will you sweeten the deal?"

The witch cocked her head with intrigue, sliding down from her pile of snakes and into the barren circle where Julia stood. Julia backed up slowly to the crystal until her back pressed against its smooth surface. The witch kinked forward until she loomed over the small girl.

"What do you have in mind?"

"I would like to be able to speak to your snakes, is all," Julia said bravely. "They scare me, but I think they would not be so scary if I could just talk to them."

The witch stood erect, satisfied. "Done!"

She snapped her fingers and Julia suddenly knew all that there was to know about plants and their powers of medicine and healing. She was also able to hear the hundreds of voices of snakes that teemed about them.

"It is hopeless."

"She should have run away. We all should have run away."

"Nothing can save the girl."

"The witch will make her into a snake like the rest of us!"

The witch cackled, her laughter drowning out the hissing of the snakes. She spun about with her arms wide, ever-powerful in her underworld domain. "What should we play first, dear Julia? What fun games do you know?"

She advanced toward Julia again.

"I know a new game," Julia beamed, reaching into her pocket. "It is called…dress-up."

"That is a funny name for a game. How do you play that?"

Julia quickly took out her *mackare*, which she had made to scare the witch away, and pulled the mask down over her face.

Upon seeing the *mackare*, crafted by the young sweet child, the witch yelped in terror. She backed away from Julia, raising her hands to shield her eyes from the visage. In desperation, and without a word, the witch flung herself down the tunnel away from Julia and the snakes.

"Hurry," Julia said to the slippery snakes. "Make a ladder and let us all escape from this terrible place!"

The snakes did as they were told, and quickly structured a ladder out of their bodies all the way to the surface world. Julia climbed as quickly as each rung was formed. After a long while, she was able to see the Old Oak and the hole through which she had fallen.

Julia climbed out into the cold snow, followed by hundreds upon hundreds of snakes.

As each snake made its way into the snow, it changed into a small child. Boys and girls of all shapes and sizes returned to their normal selves.

Upon seeing all of the poor children and knowing her parents, Julia did what any good-hearted child would. She led them away from the terrible winter and the Old Oak and took them to loving homes all over the world. She found a safe place for each child.

When spring came, Julia finally returned home with the plants she needed to help her father overcome his sickness but, to her surprise, the home was very different when she arrived.

With the witch defeated, her father's sickness was cured, and her stepmother had become as good-hearted as any folk could be. Together, the three of them lived happily ever after.

Joshua Robertson

A Simple Rose

Why ever do you try to know
the future, in which nothing is known?
Neither prophecy nor the divine can say
what will come of your fate or mine.

Stop this; don't waste your time.
For still the frost will come,
and the thunderstorms roll by.
We are drunk on summer wine.

Come, before the winter air blows.
For your life hangs like a simple rose,
drooping down for the plucking.
Take it before it goes.

A Simple Rose is another free verse without any set meter, though I have always felt its pacing fit its message. An encouraging amalgamation of words that reminds us to enjoy the moment and live our lives with liberation.

Joshua Robertson

Binding Love

You did not listen, helpless soul, when I said,
"Look out, or you'll be snagged,
You childish thing, if you dance near her hand!"

Didn't I caution you?

The snare has sprung.
To struggle is wholly hopeless.

The lust defines us, until we are caught,
And what we call love is a lie.

Entrapped, we are bound to another,
Impassioned and mindless, lost to infatuation.

Love has bound your tapping feet,
Kept you from twirling, twisting, without flow,
Chained your ankle prettily, a decorated trinket,
To be displayed as a static trophy.

Binding Love is written as a free verse from my blogging days and was inspired by a poem from antiquity that I have struggled to find ever since. The notion that we are easily enamored in our life only to find ourselves caught in less-than-fortunate situations has never escaped me. It begs the question as to what binds us up, and how we free ourselves once more.

Joshua Robertson

Ren the Red Falcon

Chapter 1

Orange flames raced across the dry grasses of the vale, lighting the darkness as it shot past the mudbrick wall around Bourhill. For generations, the Aggath slavers had defended the hill while raiding the hamlets and homesteads along the inlands and western coastline. Their soothsayers had foretold the coming of the Gruoy Shon barbarians, but no one expected the throng to come wielding fire and steel.

Helplessness ate at Ren as she peered into the darkness, unable to see the advancing barbarians in the heavy shadows. The low-hanging iron brazier above her offered a soft glow, enough to see the branches that formed the rafters of the thatch roof and the yellow hay at her feet. However, she was more interested in the distant blaze, visible through the cracked wood. She looked with wide eyes, mindlessly running her hand over her red hair, coiled on top of her head. Tucked away inside the thrall quarter—a hovel stationed in the rear of the settlement between the stockades and the stable—she knew that she and the other slaves were defenseless against the horde once they broke through the ironwood gates. Her slavers, however, would be protected within the inner walls and sanctum.

The wafting compost heap outside, filled with plant prunings and manure, stung at her senses. One of the other slaves, an olive-colored woman with raven-black hair, grabbed her pale, white shoulder and hissed with sour breath, "Let the rest of us have a look, Red Falcon. Your crooked nose has been pressed against the wall since the war horn sounded."

Frowning, Ren pulled away from the wall and clenched her fingers into a fist to keep from touching her disfigured nose, which bestowed her with the epithet *Red Falcon* for its curved shape. For as long as she could remember, the bridge of her nose had the slightest hump. She could only suspect it had been broken when she was younger, when the Aggath slavers came to take her. She could not remember most of those years, her memories washed away with the two decades of living as a thrall. Though she knew whatever beauty she might have held was taken from her.

"Innana burn you, Teyame." Ren stood, twisting her head to the left where additional slaves clustered over another hole in the wood. "Nothing can be seen out there anyhow."

With her attention off the fields, she looked for Etrium, the strongest among the slaves. She did not see him immediately. To her right, she saw Nasir and his lover, Shagshag, cowering behind the sisters, Ninsun and Meania. Sitting nearby were Iltani and Lugalme, murmuring in frightened whispers in the same fashion as the women swarming around Teyame to her left. It was not until she saw the male thralls housed with them—Adad, Pirhum, Balih—bravely hovering near the singular door leading outside that she spotted the chiseled man called Etrium. Her heart fluttered at the sight of him.

A head taller than the rest, the dark-skinned Ubaidean was said to be from a family of goat herders from the marshlands in the south near the gulf, but he had the strappings of an Aggath slaver. After a life milling grain, carrying stone, and cutting timber, he looked to have been spewed from the loins of the gods. His shoulders were twice as wide as her own; his jaw might as well have been cut from stone. The male thralls at his heel marked him as their natural leader and their best defense against the Gruoy Shon barbarians, should the enemy lift the outside bar and enter their enclosed prison.

She adjusted the pin holding her flax skirt, a finger's length above her knee, and approached Etrium. Unlike royal women, her skirts were short and she possessed no additional coverings to conceal the bareness of her arms, neck, or breasts. She thought nothing of it. Her nakedness had been forgotten years ago. No slave—female or male—wore more than the woven skirts.

"The Gruoy Shon will not slay a slave who does not fight. If victorious, they would prefer to take us to the market and sell us for profit." Etrium was speaking to the other men as she approached, emboldening his voice. "We are a treasure to be sold, not soldiers. We have nothing to fear."

"Except more slavery," Balih said.

Etrium grunted. "Do not sound so dour. Your thralldom will keep your neck uncut this day."

"We will see," Adad chuckled nervously as death cries sounded in the distance. "They may choose to only take the greatest stock to market, bearing in mind what space remains in their rolling cages. In comparison to you, Etrium, we are nothing but spoiled goods."

"They may not take us to the market at all. I heard the masters say they were in debt to the Warad-Sin." Balih lifted his finger. "We may be traded off as peace offerings."

"Not you." Adad laughed. "Only the women. The Warad-Sin are a lustful sort of men. They have no desire for anything without breasts. The more exotic, the better."

Balih glanced around the thrall quarters, catching sight of Ren. "They will find nothing exotic here."

Etrium noticeably frowned at the man.

Ren's bare foot smooshed against the rotten hay beside Balih, disregarding his searching gaze. "Do you really believe us to be safe, Etrium? Master Sidu said the barbarians were coming to punish the chief for betraying their arrangement over the Quarter-Realm." She referenced the fertile soil that separated Bourhill from the lands of the Gruoy Shon. For seven years, the sliver of cropland had been swapped every other season between the neighboring nations to keep their people fed and prosperous. After an unexpected drought, the Aggathian chief had refused this past season to relinquish their hold over the borders. "They seek to do more than shame us. Master Sidu believes they want to annihilate the Aggathians."

Etrium looked at her, a hardness on the edge of his brown eyes. "Even if they slaughter every last one, we are not Aggathians. Will they, too, slaughter the hogs and melt the silver? No, they will take their treasure to replenish their losses. I am telling you that we have nothing to fear and no reason to fight."

"We should escape while we can in the chaos," Meania said, clutching her sister's hand. She lowered her voice all the more to assure that if a guard remained outside, she would not be heard. "No living creature deserves to be locked up."

Ninsun, her sister, dipped her chin. "Given the chance, we could be across the Quarter-Realm before they know we are gone."

"And go where?" Ren asked. "Into the hands of another slaver?"

She angled her gaze at the two sisters. They were recent additions to the thrall quarters, captured after an early spring raid in the north. She had been surprised when they were brought into the camp, considering new captives were usually children; these women had as many years as Ren herself.

"Cuthah," Ninsun replied. "We would go to the city of Cuthah."

"You would join the Flame of Nergal." Ren gasped, mentioning the known cult of the underworld god.

"They would protect us from the slavers and the barbarians." Meania lifted her finger at Ren as though it were a knife. The black-skinned woman's sudden expression was haunting, her dark eyes seeming to widen, the whites growing.

Ren's own deity, Innana—a goddess of beauty and warfare—would never permit her to step foot into Nergal's domain willingly, unless she were seeking to destroy her shadow self to become purer before reaching the life hereafter. The perilous journey sounded less than agreeable to Ren. She would never bend the knee to Nergal.

"The lot of you speak as though our masters are fools." Teyame turned in their direction, abandoning her post where Ren kept watch moments ago. The vixen almost shouted at the sisters, though her darting eyes included Ren in her venomous accusation, while she pushed her hair violently from her cheek. She dared look at Etrium as she went on, silently grouping him among them. "Our masters will stomp the Gruoy Shon, and then you will be flogged for your scheming. No matter your worth, they will whip you for speaking ill of them."

He did not miss the implication. "Do not fault me for giving council to my brothers," he said. "I do not speak words of treachery!"

Teyame scowled. "We will see how they judge your words, mighty Etrium."

Ren did not bother asking how they would learn of whispers among thralls. No doubt Teyame would be the one who told the slavers of any who spoke against them, bending the truth to serve her own purpose. She always sought an opportunity to gain favor, thinking she might advance to a maidservant among the richer wives.

A slaver outside stomped by the door, shouting, "Fall back! They are over the walls!"

Ren stepped back as another pair of footsteps approached. The bar of the door thudded to the dirt outside and the door was thrown open. She recognized Master Sidu's wrinkled cheeks above his swollen chest as he lifted an obsidian-tipped spear at them. The silver earrings beneath his copper helmet glimmered in the light of the braziers. "We need more bodies. Come with me," he said, his gray beard waggling. "All of you."

"We are not warriors," Balih protested from between Ren and Etrium, shrinking back with trembling hands. Cries of war echoed somewhere in the distance.

"You are whatever I say you are. Now come!" Master Sidu lobbed the spear at him.

Balih lifted his hands to keep the weapon from smacking him in the face, but Ren was quicker, reaching out and catching it in the air. Her chest filled with sudden heat, gripping the smooth stave in her long fingers. She had never wielded a spear before, but the weight felt natural in her hand.

She locked her jaw to keep her surprise from escaping her lips in an elevated whine, noticing the other thralls gaping at her swift movement. Etrium's eyes stayed on her the longest.

Lifting an eyebrow, Master Sidu cleared his throat and stepped out of the doorframe. He motioned with his thick hand for them to exit the hut, squinting at Ren. "The rest of you gather weapons from Master Iddin up the street." Etrium led the way out, towering over the Aggathian with the rest of the thralls funneling behind. As Ren exited, Master Sidu glowered, saying, "And unless you wish to lose your hands, you will keep the sharp end pointed at the enemy."

Chapter 2

The barbarians were pushing up the center of the road when Ren and the others were finally led away from Master Iddin with weapons in hand. She still clutched the spear, chewing on her bottom lip in anticipation of the fight to come, as they clustered together in the street.

"Stand shoulder to shoulder across this road," Master Sidu instructed angrily, pulling them away from one another so they might have space to swing their blades. He did not even look at Ren as he shoved her between Teyame and Balih, each holding a thin sword half as long as their arms. He shook his finger at them, finishing his lecture by pointing at the mudbrick wall behind them. "Do not let a single one of those curs pass. You must hold them until we prepare the defenses on the inner wall. If you try to flee, our archers will let loose their arrows on you!"

No one said a word as Master Sidu continued to threaten them, glancing over his shoulder at the coming Gruoy Shon. In the fire-lit streets, Ren could make out several dozen among the advancing army. Their double-sided axes, oversized swords, and glistening shields looked imposing when compared to her and her companions' half-sized armaments. She feared they would be cut down like summer's crop, having no skill with the blades or armor to protect their own flesh.

Next thing Ren knew, Ninsun was murmuring farther down the line. "We are nothing more than bodies to them. We will be dead whether we stand and fight or not."

Ren jerked her head around to see Master Sidu scrambling to the secondary walls, waving to the men on the ramparts to open the gate.

"We should run," Meania said. "Are you with us, Red Falcon?"

Etrium stepped out of the line and narrowed his eyes at them. "If we run, we are all dead. We stand a better chance sticking together."

Adad and Pirhum grunted in agreement behind him and lifted their blades.

"I agree with you," Teyame said.

"We cannot fight them!" Balih cried. Before he could be stopped, he spun around and dashed after Master Sidu, screaming loud enough that his voice cracked. "Let us inside, masters. We cannot serve you out here!"

The arrow that zipped from the walkway above the wall and into Balih's chest was swift. He dropped to his side, releasing his thin sword, and folded over to the dirt to accept his death with as much fight as Ren would expect. He did not even bother to reach for the arrow lodged in his torso.

"We fight!" Etrium roared, turning away from the deserter to face the oncoming barbarians.

Ren bent her legs, palms strangely dry against the smooth wood of the spear. The barbarians matched Etrium's shout, stomping up the road in unison, slamming their weapons against their shields. Sweat glinted on their chests with droplets lacing their long beards. Ren saw some were bleeding from the invasion; most were not.

"Innana, make my skin as stone," Ren quietly prayed as the barbarians stampeded at them like wild horses.

Etrium bravely charged at them, madly waving his large sword to slap away the blade of the first enemy and then fending back two more. Adad hurtled forward with the larger thrall, cutting the neck of the first barbarian as he tried to regain his balance after clashing with Etrium's brawn.

Ren heard two thralls scream as they were cut down. Unwilling to turn her attention from the Gruoy Shon hurrying toward her, she could not see who fell. By the sound, she could not even say whether they were male or female. With Balih gone, Ren was sandwiched between Teyame and Shagshag, neither giving her much room to move the spear. She took a single step back as the first barbarian reached them.

His steel ax dropped down to be deflected simultaneously by Shagshag's and Teyame's swords. Without thinking, Ren's muscles tensed and then hurried to extend her arms, stabbing the tip of her spear into the soft flesh under the barbarian's arm. He jerked away and tripped while trying to keep his balance. Crimson bled down his side and he disappeared behind the throng of his brethren.

"Well done." Teyame clicked her tongue, examining Ren. "Maybe you are not completely useless, Red Falcon."

"She fights like a spear-maiden from Nanna Valley," Shagshag hurried to say.

Teyame scoffed. "Stabbing a man in the armpit does not bequeath her the title of spear-maiden. Besides, those tribes were wiped from existence years ago."

"No," Shagshag said. "It is in her blood."

A flash of red sparked in Ren's mind, igniting a memory and words to flow from her dry tongue. She choked, "Actually, I think my mother was a spear-maiden."

"What?" Teyame gaped.

Three massive men stopped just short of them, causing Ren to hold her tongue. She was not sure what more she could say anyway. Her thoughts were a whirlwind, unclear. She thought she remembered her mother holding a spear, but so much was forgotten.

The slavers made them forget. Her childhood was a dream.

One of the barbarians neared while the battle clashed around them on the streets. Ren saw Etrium continuing to fight behind them, Adad already lying dead. The barbarian drew her attention, smirking. "Did they honestly send women to protect them from our wrath?"

"Look like peace offerings to me." The second snorted, ogling Ren and licking his lips.

"They are slaves. I have no desire to harm a woman," the third said. He shook his head with indifference. His thick black hair was held in place by his domed helmet but long enough to cover his eyes. "Lay down your weapons and we will return for you when we are done with your masters."

"I want this one," the second said, motioning to Ren.

"She is ugly," the first replied, "but I suppose they all look the same from the rear."

The second one elbowed the first. "She will look different with that red hair painting her back. How long do you think her hair is?"

Ren swallowed hard.

The dark-haired barbarian shushed them with a growl, and then said, "I will not tell you again. Lay down your weapons or you will bleed alongside your masters."

Ren hesitated, her heart thudding against her breast.

Before she could decide how to react, Shagshag dropped her sword and fell to her knees while Teyame lunged at the barbarians. The first barbarian smacked away her sword with his metal bracer and then slit her stomach open in a fluid motion. Warm blood splashed across the road, spraying the tops of Ren's bare feet.

As though the decision was made for her, strength was sapped from her knees as she dropped the spear and bowed to the barbarians. From the corner of her eye, she watched Teyame slosh bloody spit from her trembling lips and slump to the street.

The raven-haired thrall met Ren's eyes. "You…are…no spear-maiden." She garbled again, her lifeless eyes turning to the heavens.

"Stay put. You now belong to Inkish," the third barbarian ordered, stepping between Ren and Shagshag. The clanging of metal on metal sounded on either side as the few remaining thralls fought against the horde. Ren was fearful to see if Etrium was still on his feet.

"I want a run at the redhead—" the second tried again.

"You will speak to Inkish," the third cut in, turning his head, "before you receive any prize."

A bellow from Ren's left indicated Nasir, Shagshag's lover, had chosen not to submit to the barbarians with ease. His sword tore through the darkness over Shagshag's bent form, striking the third barbarian. The blade slipped under the helmet and into his neck before being ripped free with equal swiftness.

Nasir recklessly spun around to face the other two. He'd barely raised the weapon for another attack when the barbarians' axes came down on either side and hacked through muscle and sinew. His death screams were fragmented, fading to silence as he collapsed, his dead body curling like a shell over Shagshag. She pushed Nasir to the side, trying to stand while ducking under the swinging blades.

"No! Curse you! No!" She wept, folding her arms over her breasts and holding her face.

Ren twisted to look at Shagshag, wanting to comfort her or stand and fight again, but the goddess, Innana, seemed to keep her cowering. The twang of bows snapping loose from ramparts was followed by a dozen arrows, several of which pierced through Shagshag and the first barbarian. Ren buried her head instead of watching the thrall die and reached for the spear at her side.

More screams echoed around her as another canopy of arrows rained down on slaves and enemies alike. The Aggath slavers meant to slaughter them all.

She had to run.

"Come with me!" Etrium's deep tone reached her ear. His meaty hand grabbed her under the arm in an attempt to pull her to her feet. Ren heard a pained grunt accompany his effort. Footsteps slapped against the ground on either side as she faltered to her feet. "We must find a place to hide."

Lifting her eyes to Etrium, she could see the deep gashes on his chest, arms, and legs. She did not expect him to survive until morning.

"No," Meania said with her sister at her side. She looked over her shoulder at the barbarians advancing on the sanctum. "Now is our chance to flee. Come with us, Red Falcon, and be a slave no more."

Ren dropped her gaze to the dead strewn over the ground and realized every thrall was gone but the four of them. She was surprised that any of them survived, save Etrium.

"We should not leave Bourhill," Etrium said. "We will be punished. We can hide and wait until the Aggathians or Gruoy Shon are victorious, and then bend the knee. Come with me, Ren, and live another day."

More barbarians were coming through the gates.

Ren gripped the spear in her hand, feeling something stir inside her, something long forgotten.

She looked to Etrium apologetically. "I cannot."

Chapter 3

Ren rested on the thick grasses of the Quarter-Realm, soaking in the warmth of the sun. Not far away, a stream trickled through the valley where it fed into a river farther to the south. A few droplets remained on her lips from drinking her fill a moment ago. She could not remember when she was able to drink so freely without worrying about being reprimanded or whipped for not returning swiftly enough to her labor.

While the night had been full of trepidation, running, and fumbling through the dark in desperation to escape Bourhill, the day had been slow-moving and without worry. The images of mayhem and bloodshed flashed indistinctly whenever she closed her eyes, devoid of any real meaning or emotion. Her dead masters and fellow thralls held as much meaning in her life as the horse manure she had been forced to clear from the roads. In time, she thought it all might be forgotten. That is, except for Teyame's final words, *you are no spear-maiden.*

The words stung and she knew not why.

Meania and Ninsun returned from the water's edge and squatted down on the grass beside her. Ninsun tugged at her wild, stringy hair. "I do not know how you survived all those years as a slave, Red Falcon. Another cycle of the moon and I would have surely taken my own life."

"You would have left me?" Meania asked her sister almost teasingly, tongue clicking before she spoke.

Ninsun shrugged. "Nothing stopping you from following me. Nergal would not have faulted you. Serving anyone but yourself is a death sentence anyhow."

Ren raised an eyebrow, hearing the name of the underworld god once more. The sisters were set on traveling to Cuthah to join the Flame of Nergal.

"Does Innana see taking your own life differently?" Meania asked her, seeming to notice her reaction. "When might it be permissible?"

"I have never thought about it," Ren admitted, sitting up to meet her dark eyes. "Serving the Aggathians was simply how things were and always have been. I never thought it honorable to take my own life."

"Is that something your mother taught you?" Meania frowned.

"I don't really remember."

"No honor in a slave's life," Ninsun said.

"Perhaps you are right." Ren sucked in a mouthful of cool air and slowly exhaled, digesting the comment. She crossed her legs and softened her features, saying, "This is nice, though. I am not sure I have ever taken a breath for myself."

"You were not born into slavery, were you?" Ninsun asked. Ren shook her head. "I thought not. You have the fiery hair and ashen skin of the Nanna Valley people."

Snapping her attention to the younger sister, Ren's mouth dried at the silent implication. "I thought they were all dead."

"The spear-maidens are," she replied, "if that is what you are referring to, but plenty of people still roam in the Nanna Valley. Their red hair and pale skin are no different than your own. From what I know, any who survived the raids of the slavers were swallowed up by the other tribes."

Ren swallowed, shaking her head gently. "Survived? No one survived."

"Something always survives," Meania replied.

The dull thudding of hoofbeats sounded in the distance, growing louder from whence they had come. Ren was the first to her feet, grabbing the obsidian-tipped spear lying on the ground next to her and facing the mounting cacophony. A train of riders, shouting and clanking on the backs of their steeds, rode at a brisk gallop in their direction. Lances, axes, shields, and steel caps rattled as they extended forward in a single line. The dozen riders did not slow, even when the lead horseman leaned forward to examine the grasses in front of him, all the while kicking the sides of his mount.

Ren gawked at the black and yellow colors of his cloak fluttering over the horse's flank, following the attire to his bodily form when she heard him shout. "There!" The Gruoy Shon barbarian pointed at her, the matted black hair on either side of his sun-crisped face looking somewhat familiar at the distance. "Onward! Bring them back!"

"They have come for us," Meania whispered in disbelief.

"Why would they?" her sister gaped. "Why would the barbarians care about a few thralls?"

"I do not know. Come on!" Meania pulled at Ren's shoulder.

Ren tightened her grip on the spear, the butt of the weapon fastened to the ground like an oversized stone. She looked to the unmarked path winding along the river and then the open field surrounding them. The inevitability of being captured again caused her head to spin. "Where would we run? We cannot outrun the horses."

"The river! We will swim across," Meania said.

Ren caught her breath, eyeing the rushing river. She did not know how to swim.

Before she could respond, Meania and Ninsun flung themselves into the river, flailing against the broken waters in attempts to cross to the other side. The waves swelled over their heads in sporadic movements, lapping over their kicking legs and flapping arms.

The horses thundered on either side of Ren, drumming to a halt as the barbarian roared to the company, "Stop them!"

The twang of bowstrings resounded, followed by several feathered arrows plunging into the waters around the two dark-skinned sisters. Ren squinted to see if any met their mark when a brown steed moved into her peripheral view.

"Throw down your weapon, thrall."

Ren immediately tossed the spear to the dirt and kneeled in panic, a plea spilling from her lips in a near whimper. "Spare me, please."

"I said you belonged to Inkish," he replied. Ren dared to turn her head, now recognizing the dome helmet of the black-haired barbarian she crossed at Bourhill. "Who did your masters send you to fetch?"

Ren tightened her lips and wrinkled her brow at the barbarian on his mount as another set of arrows hummed into the river after the sisters. They thought she, Meania, and Ninsun were sent to call on allies of the Aggathians, of which there were none. She hurried to calculate whether her punishment would be lessened if she were on an errand for the slavers instead of trying to escape. Her tongue searched for the name of any nearby tribe or settlement and found no believable name worth mentioning.

"Loosen your tongue, woman," he growled. "Where are they running off to?"

Ren beheld Meania and Ninsun crawling along the rocky shoreline on the opposite side of the river. Ninsun was first to find her footing and twisted to help her sister ashore, all the while eyeing Ren across the expanse. More arrows were loosed, wildly striking beyond the scope of the women; Meania and Ninsun had made the swim and were safe. Ren would have followed them had she not been fearful of drowning in the attempt.

"They are going to Cuthah," Ren said.

"Cuthah?" he repeated, and then directed his companions with a savage bark. "Hold your fire." He studied Ren, intermittently casting a glance to the two escaping farther down the river. He squinted ever so slightly, almost with amusement. When he finally spoke, his tongue was laced with what appeared to be delight. "The punishment for desertion is death. I am sure that you already know this, thrall. You must have thought yourself to be brave, scarpering off into the unknown amidst the battle."

"Anything but, milord. I was fearful with the arrows being loosed on us and screams of the dying around me," she started. Her chest swelled with her beating heart, the desire for life warming her with every word. Ren fought not to take notice of the spear resting a fingertip's length away. She knew fighting the entire company would be impossible for a seasoned spear-maiden, let alone a slave with a spear. "Spare me, please," she managed to beg.

"Your fate is not mine to decide," he said. "We will take you to Inkish."

Chapter 4

Cold stars gleamed above by the time they were snaking up the path to Bourhill. Ren's hands were bound, the line of rope held by the dark-haired barbarian who had captured her. With her head hung low, the obsidian-tipped spear was visible, bouncing over his saddle, taunting her. She should have never thrown it away.

Her goddess gave her strength one moment and weakened her the next. She did not understand why she would be allowed to flee from her prison only to be dragged back again. Her voice was meek against the sound of clopping hooves. "What do you desire of me, Innana? Tell me, am I meant to be enslaved or free?"

"What are you going on about back there?" an adjacent barbarian barked, scowling under a mountain of facial hair. He spat at her feet when she did not answer, droplets catching on his beard. Clamping her lips together, her attention drifted to the mudbrick walls of Bourhill coming into focus ahead of her, standing torches spotting either end of the rocky road. From the walls, she could see several bodies hanging, long dead, gutted and swollen with the ropes fastened under their arms and around their chests instead of lassoed around the neck. In fact, upon closer inspection, she saw many of the corpses did not even have their heads. The gaping faces, dripping entrails, were instead positioned on steel pikes outside the gates as though they warned others what reward awaited those who double-crossed the Gruoy Shon.

As she passed under the gates, one ghastly head caught her eye, staring at her with a fallen jaw and lifeless eyes. Master Sidu.

She wondered if Etrium's head also decorated the end of a pike.

Stifling a gasp, she averted her eyes to see the smoldering fires of leveled homes. Many continued to crackle, the gray and black smoke billowing toward the moonless sky. The livestock had been corralled into a single corner of the settlement, while a handful of Aggathians left alive were pushed to another. Ren guessed they would be sold into slavery themselves, if not slaughtered. In the center of the path, leading to the sanctum, silver, weapons, and other treasures were piled up for the taking.

Stopping next to the plunder, the barbarian climbed down from his saddle, careful to balance Ren's spear in his hand. He rushed straight to the inner sanctum, using her weapon as a walking stick and tugging on the rope so she would follow. "Take my horse. I will bring her to Inkish."

A man at Ren's rear grunted in acknowledgement.

In all her years, Ren had only stepped foot in the sanctum twice. Once upon her capture and the second when she had come with Teyame to deliver a batch of honeyed wine during a celebration several years back. At the time, she had been impressed at the luxury and comfort of the halls. Woven rugs, jeweled vases, bronze braziers, and hung tapestries were among the many riches to be found, but now the sanctum was emptied, a bleak shell of what the Aggathians had created on the shoulders of their slaves.

The sound of her footsteps slapped against the stone floors echoed in unison with the barbarian's clanking boots as they ambled down the wide hall to the open chamber ahead. The deep baritone of multiple men arguing echoed off the stoned pillars that mirrored one another on either side of the walking path. Ren could not understand the heated words, as the men ahead spoke over one another. Instead, she concentrated on the etchings in the rock. Faces meant to represent the gods were carved from floor to ceiling in the thick walls. She looked for Innana but was not sure she would recognize her goddess's image if she found it.

"He will fetch us plenty of silver."

"Hardly. He is hanging on by a thread of life as we speak. Leave him to die or cut his throat but let us be done with it."

"I agree. We should not be debating over the life of a thrall. We have plenty of prisoners to take to market without dragging this hunk of meat along with us."

"But I have...bent the knee!"

The dissonance of multiple voices boomed one after another off the walls, amplified by the lack of furnishings in the chamber. Three armored men, one with a feathered helm, stood around the burly thrall, his long dark hair canopying his bloodied shoulders. Ren recognized Etrium. He should have never survived with his wounds, and yet here he was before her. A strange sense of relief washed over Ren for reasons she did not quite understand; her outbreath was louder than intended, escaping from the depths of her throat as though she had been holding it since leaving him behind. If her hands were not bound, she may have covered her lips. Instead, she hung her head as though nothing transpired, telling herself she was glad his head was not on a pike.

He seemed not to notice her, cowering in the middle of the three Gruoy Shon. His muscles quaked in his back, his wounds seeping and dried blood caking his flesh.

Ren bit her bottom lip, approaching Etrium from the rear. Did Innana bring her back to save Etrium? Was he meant to be free with her? What did Innana want from her?

Before she was able to utter a prayer, the barbarian with the feathered helm lifted his eyes to face them, revealing his scarred face, painted black and yellow like her captor's cloak. "What have you brought me, Koth?"

The dark-haired barbarian removed his helm, jerking Ren closer to him with the rope. She stumbled and fell to her knees at his heel. "We pursued the thrall women as you asked. Two fled across the river, but we retrieved this one. She claims they were running away to Cuthah and *not* summoning more warriors for the slavers. I think she is telling the truth."

"Cuthah? The city is in the far east. Quite far for a handful of slaves to run," the man who Ren guessed to be Inkish replied. He crossed his arms, narrowing his eyes at Ren and chuckled to himself. "Were you taken by her shape? Maybe she is a witch and cast some spell over you."

"I am not so easily swayed," Koth said.

"Perhaps you are hoping to escape my wrath for letting the other two go free." Inkish hummed, holding the smirk on his lips and tucking his hairless chin to his chest. "Why did you not chase them across the river, or at least send a few of your men to cut them down?"

"She is…not lying," Etrium interrupted.

Inkish lost his smile and looked at the wavering thrall at his feet. "Excuse me?"

Etrium slowly glanced over his shoulder at Ren, his features gripped with exhaustion and pain. His voice rasped with each word. "Her name is Red Falcon. The women you speak of discussed running to Cuthah before you broke through the gates. They knew you would defeat the Aggathians. Red Falcon would not aid the slavers."

Ren tightened her hands around her end of her bindings. She had to save him.

Koth thinned his lips and brushed his hair out of his eyes, slackening the rope. "There you have it."

"You are too trusting, Koth," Inkish said.

"Kill them both and let us go home," the barbarian to Etrium's left said, pulling at the braided tassels of his beard.

The remaining barbarian tucked his fingers in the sides of his britches. "I say throw them in with the rest and let's sell them at the market."

Inkish pushed past Etrium, leaving him with the two nameless Gruoy Shon, and approached Ren. He stood over her and consumed her with his eyes, licking his lips in thought. "I have a better idea. Because of these inbred bastards, we owe the Warad-Sin for their aid this past season. We might as well deliver this young beauty to them. What do you think, Koth? Is she pretty enough?"

"I do not care what you do with her, Inkish," the dark-haired barbarian said.

The man from the left of Etrium snorted. "She looks ugly to me. What is wrong with her nose?"

"Bah! No one asked you," Inkish snapped, looking over his shoulder. "Kill that thrall already. We are taking her to the Warad-Sin."

"No!" Ren's scream was otherworldly, her muscles moving against her will as though they were haunted by the spear-maidens of Nanna Valley or Innana herself. Ren rolled back and sideways around Koth and sprung to her feet, pulling on her bindings with all her strength, catching the taut rope behind his knees. He cried out in surprise, dropping his helm and the obsidian-tipped spear simultaneously while landing flat on his back.

Ren snatched the spear, still bound at her wrists, and twisted the weapon so the shaft was tucked under her arm; the tip floated in line with Inkish's painted chin. His mouth opened to protest and Ren did not hesitate. With terrible swiftness, she thrust the end through his open mouth and out the rear of his neck.

Her strength shocked her. Innana stood with her.

Steel ripped from scabbards on either side of Etrium, followed by the hollow gasps of the unnamed dogs standing over him. Ren pulled her weapon free, unleashing a battle cry to wilt daisies when the cord around her arms was jerked by Koth. Her bold yell was reduced to a squawk as she was pulled off her feet and reeled into the thick arms of her subjugator. The spear fell away, clanking against the stone tiles, as Koth released the coil of rope to wrestle her to the ground with him.

"What have you done?" he shouted from beneath her, locking his grip around her waist.

His answer was lost to the bellow of the barbarians crossing the brawn of Etrium. Her heroism somehow sparked vigor into the mighty thrall. In her struggle against Koth, she glimpsed one falling away with his sword wedged in his throat, and the other received a massive fist in the chest, which hammered the air from his lungs. The bastard lurched back into the wall while Etrium reached for the first's sword.

Their victory was at hand.

Ren's skin was on fire, her muscles red-hot in her effort to break free. The goddess of war and beauty was with her; she felt her guiding hand. Through gritted teeth, Ren prayed, "Make my skin as stone, Innana."

Ren threw her head back and smashed into Koth's nose, silencing whatever words had started spilling from his lips again. The satisfying crunch was followed by his loosened grip. Kicking off his thigh with her bare foot, she had the momentum to roll from his body, luckily landing in proximity to the spear. She scrambled to clasp the weapon between her thin fingers, rotating on her heel to face Koth again.

His mop of black hair covered his eyes, blood streaming from his shattered nose. With flailing hands, half tangled in rope, Koth elevated his head in time to hear the death cry of the brute facing Etrium. His eye darted to Ren, focusing on the obsidian tip aligned with his left eye.

"You do not have to kill me. I will let you go," he stammered. "I swear to you."

Ren's jaw tremored. "Horses?"

"Choose any that you like. You can have mine if you want it."

"Food? Medicine?"

"It is yours," he replied. "Our fight was never with you."

She nodded and lowered her spear.

Etrium stumbled forward a step before sinking to a knee at her side. He weakly lifted his sword at Koth before dropping his arm to his side. "You are…fierce, Red Falcon. The blood of the spear-maidens flows through you." He coughed. "Now what will you do?"

"I will leave this place and this time, you will come with me. Come, our freedom awaits."

Together they made their way to mounts and rode away from Bourhill. With a wild smile on her face, Ren gripped the mane of the horse beneath her. Only destiny lay ahead.

Drunken Poet

If you find a poet's poem,
written but undefined,
without the final line,
it is likely the poet's home,
tasteful but unrefined,
is fortified with wine!

Drunken Poet is a free verse with a set meter and one of my latest writings in the genre of poetry. This has always been one of the favorites that I penned. While I have never claimed it to have great meaning, it is a token of my appreciation for alcohol and its impact on writing well or not at all.

Joshua Robertson

The Fifth Brother

A long time ago, there was a story of a huntsman who had four sons who wanted to go and gain experience in the world, but that was not the whole story. Perhaps, you don't know the story even as it was told. Here, let me tell you again and then tell you the part that has been hidden from you.

Four sons were born to a huntsman and when they were all over the age of sixteen, they said to their father, "We are going into the world, but we need money for our journey. Please take what you have from your savings and let us explore so that we, too, can become men."

Knowing their wisdom to be true, the huntsman acquiesced to his sons' requests. He gave them each one hundred silver and a horse apiece.

The four sons mounted their horses, took their coins, and rode from their home in the forest to the mountains. Within the mountains, they came to a crossroads with a path leading in each direction, and in the middle of the intersection stood a beech tree.

The eldest stopped them and said, "Brothers, this is where we separate to go out and find our fortune in the world. Take your knife and stick it in this tree, and in a year and a day let us all come here together again. These knives will be our tokens. If ever one of the knives becomes rusty, then we will know that the one to whom it belongs will be dead. And for any whose knife is free from rust, we will know them to be alive and well."

And then the four brothers separated and went their own way. They each came to a suitable place where they could grow into a man and learn a handicraft. The eldest learned to be a tinkerer, the second learned to be a thief, the third learned to be an astrologer, and the fourth learned to be a huntsman like their father.

Once a year and a day had passed, the four brothers started on their return. The eldest was the first to arrive at the beech tree, where he pulled out his own knife and saw the other knives were free from rust.

He rejoiced, saying, "Praise to the four winds, we are all alive and well," and he rode onward to his father's home.

When he arrived, his father said to him, "I can see that you have become a man. What manner of handicraft have you learned?"

The son replied, "Father, it is no use but to tell you the truth: I'm a tinkerer."

"That is a fine profession to have."

"But, father, I'm not a tinkerer like other tinkerers. I'm a tinkerer that can take anything worn out and say, 'let it be mended up,' and it is so at once."

The father fetched a worn coat he owned which the elbows had all but worn away. He handed it to his son, who gave the command, "Let it be mended up." At that moment, the coat was mended up as if it were newly made. The father said nothing more, in awe of his son's craft.

The next day, the second son came to the beech tree. He pulled out his own knife and looked at the remaining two. Seeing that they were both free from rust, he rejoiced, and said, "Praise be to the four winds! We are all alive and well; our eldest brother is at home already."

He went home. When he came to his father, his father said to him, "I can see that you have become a man. What manner of handicraft have you learned?"

The son replied, "Father, it is no use but to tell you the truth: I'm a thief."

"That is a gainful trade, but wicked to be. Shame on you!"

"But, father, I'm not a thief like other thieves. I'm a thief that can think of anything, no matter where it is and with a thought, I have it with me at once."

At that moment, a jackrabbit came running over the hillside and could be seen through the window. The father told his second son to fetch the creature. His son immediately said, "Let yon jackrabbit be here," and it was with them at once. The father said nothing more, in awe of his son's craft.

On the third day, the third son came to the beech tree. He pulled out his own knife and looked at the remaining one. Seeing it was free from rust, he rejoiced and said, "Praise be to the four winds! We are all alive and well; my two elder brothers are at home already."

He went home. When he came to his father, his father said to him, "I can see that you have become a man. What manner of handicraft have you learned?"

The son replied, "Father, it is no use but to tell you the truth: I'm an astrologer."

"That is a nice handicraft."

"But, father, I'm an astrologer who, if I look at the sky, I can at once see where anything is in the whole earth. I can tell you that our fourth brother will be here tomorrow." The father said nothing more, in awe of his son's craft.

On the fourth day, the youngest son came to the beech tree. He pulled out his own knife and looked to see the other three missing. He was glad and said, "My brothers are already all at home."

He went home. When he came to his father, his father said to him, "I can see that you have become a man. What manner of handicraft have you learned?"

The son replied, "Father, it is no use but to tell you the truth: I'm a huntsman."

"You have followed the steps of your father, and for that, you're a good lad."

"But, father, I'm not such a huntsman as you. If I come across a head of game, I say, 'Let it be shot', and immediately shot it is."

At that moment, a jackrabbit came running over the hillside and could be seen through the window. The father told his second son to shoot the creature. His son immediately spoke the words and the hare lay dead.

The father said, "I don't see whether it is lying dead."

The astrologer looked to the sky and said, "Yes, father. It's lying there behind the bushes."

"How do we get it?" the father asked.

The second son said, "Let it be here." Immediately, there it was, but it had come through thorny bushes and was all torn.

The father said, "The whole skin is torn. No one would buy it from us."

The eldest brother said, "Let it be mended up." Immediately, it was mended up. The father said nothing more, in awe of his sons' handicrafts.

For some time, they lived with their father and maintained themselves well with their handicrafts. Until came the day they heard news from an adjacent land. A wealthy king made a proclamation that to whomever should find his lost daughter, the princess, he would give her hand and his kingdom as well.

The four brothers said to one another, "Let us go and rescue this princess and gain our due reward. We are masters of our handicrafts and together we can make a name for ourselves and no longer live as simple men in the forest with our father."

Their father did not give them leave to go, but they left anyway to find the lost princess. When they came to the king, they confirmed that he had made the promise to give his daughter's hand and the Kingdom to whomever would find her.

He said this was the truth and cried, "Tell me, where is my daughter being held?"

The astrologer replied, "Your poor daughter has been taken captive by a dragon and is being held on an island beyond the sea. She is being forced to please him for two hours every day with the sound of her voice. For the rest of the time, the dragon has his head placed upon her lap, allowing her to do nothing else except eat and sleep."

"Please, save her," the king pleaded to the brothers.

The following day, the brothers assembled a carriage and headed to the edge of the sea. They then got into a boat and rode to the island where the princess was being held. When arriving on the coast, they saw the Princess out walking because the dragon was not home. But the astrologer knew that he was flying home and they were in danger. He told his brothers they must move swiftly.

The thief called out, "Let the princess be here!" She was in the boat with them at once, but the dragon came over the ridge, full of wrath, and roared as he rose above them in the air.

The astrologer said to the huntsman, "Brother, shoot him."

The huntsman said, "Let him be shot." Immediately, the dragon was shot but fell on the boat and cracked it so that water flooded its base.

The brothers threw the dragon into the sea. Then the tinkerer said, "Mend the leak," and not a drop of water came into the boat again.

The four brothers then arrived safely with the princess, taking her in the carriage and returning her to the king and her kingdom. They disputed as to which one of them would take her hand in marriage and to whom the kingdom would belong.

The astrologer said, "The princess is mine. If it hadn't been for me, we wouldn't have known where the Princess could be found."

"No, the princess is mine," said the thief. "If it hadn't been for me, we wouldn't have gotten her into the boat."

"Surely, the princess is mine," said the huntsman. "It is I that slew the dragon and truly saved us from death."

"If it hadn't been for me, we would have drowned and perished," the eldest claimed. "And, of course, I am the oldest. I think the princess is mine."

When they came to the palace, they asked the king to decide to whom the Princess would belong. The king said, "While you all deserve her, you all cannot have her. My proclamation was that whomever should find her would gain her hand and the kingdom. It was the astrologer who found her and he alone will have her. However, all of you should be rewarded with your own districts in the kingdom."

In this, they were all content. After the wedding, their father was brought to the kingdom and he was thrilled that his sons were men, masters of their handicrafts and with wealth and titles to their name.

And this is the story, as most know, but now we should tell the final part that has been hidden from you. What is not told is the story of the mysterious fifth brother, the son of the father and the harlot, whom the other brothers had never known.

After the dragon was slain, the brothers had lived happily in their districts, showered with gifts and riches and beautiful wives. Their father traveled to each of his four sons' homes at each season to live a happy life, rejoicing in the success of his sons.

After a short time, the father said to himself, "I have had four sons who have all brought blessings upon my house and upon my name. I am nearing old age and I am deserving of more blessings yet. I should have another son to increase my joy."

The father no longer had a wife, who had died a number of years ago, and he set out to find the woman who might carry a fifth son. After proposing his intended plan to several women and being turned down more times than he could count, the father became discouraged. That is until a woman at an alehouse told him that she desperately wanted a child. She offered to birth his child for a bit of coin if they remained unwed, and he if remained absent from the child's life until adulthood.

The father agreed, feeling as though he had no other choice. The father had no issue in paying the woman for her deed, as each of his other sons was rich and gave him money freely.

The deed was done, and the father did not come to the alehouse anymore. Before his youngest son reached adulthood, on his deathbed, he told the eldest son, the tinkerer, of what he had done.

The eldest son vowed to find his littlest brother and quickly met with his other younger brothers that were still monarchs in their districts. Upon hearing the news, the astrologer said, "find him," and shared that the fifth brother was still at the alehouse, full of grief from the life that he had endured. The brothers set off to meet their youngest sibling with hopes of showering the boy, who was clearly a pauper, with the riches of their family.

Along the path, the brothers were met by a gang of bandits. The bandits threatened to kill them and their horses if they did not turn over their riches. The huntsman, thinking of his little brother's woe, did not want to be delayed by the bandits. He commanded justice and said, "kill it", and they all fell dead.

On the second day, when stopping for a midday meal, the horses became spooked and fled away from the camp. The brothers rushed to grab the reins but were unsuccessful as horses can gallop quite quickly. The tinkerer, huntsman, and astrologer became panicked as the horses increased their distance from the camp. The thief simply smiled at his brothers and said, "take them," and the horses were back at the brothers' side. Together, they continued their journey.

On the third day, at the alehouse, the pauper agreed to meet with the four brothers and listen to the story of their father. The pauper responded by saying, "My mother died in birthing me and I have always wondered who my father was that abandoned me. I do not know whether your story brings me joy or pain, but my heart breaks in sadness."

The tinkerer said, "mend it," and the fifth brother's heart was whole. The pauper soon found himself overwhelmed with happiness and joy that had never been known before. He welcomed the riches of his brothers and embraced them as kin.

"What manner of handicraft have you learned?" the astrologer asked him.

The fifth brother replied, "My brothers, it is no use but to tell you the truth: I'm a minstrel. Though, I am not like any other minstrel. Whenever I say, 'sing it,' my song is heard by the whole world."

And the minstrel did just that, telling the story of his four brothers that had lifted him from his despair into gladness. From that time forward, the five brothers brought more blessings to their house and to their name.

Joshua Robertson

Response to Thrasymachus

Speak in whispers, foolish Thrasymachus,
Socrates will hear your weak argument,
You bravely refute the worth of justice,
The audience sees you as abhorrent.

Claim that being unjust is a virtue,
Once more, living justly is but a vice,
Poor Sophist, however can you be true?
When a logic of evil you entice.

How trouble-free it is for a fair man,
To choose when his craft is rightly precise,
Saying, when he fails again and again,
The artistry is not his. O' how wise.

Alas, this freewill lets you choose your part,
You draw but what you see, know not the heart.

Response to Thrasymachus was one of many attempts at a Shakespearean sonnet though I am not confident I mastered iambic pentameter. Regardless, I frequently read Plato's Republic in my early 20s and thought it enjoyable to craft this poem as a response. Thrasymachus argued that "might makes right", whereas Socrates argued that a good ruler has an interest in the interests of his subjects.

Dishonored Prometheus

Ascend to Mount Caucasus, and witness Prometheus,
Aloneness fulfills his heart; Ethon predates his poor
pate,
A sedate nature held for the striking sire of the fire,
The choir denotes a fate for his courage judged amiss.

Hubris! Zeus's disgust for mankind's undying prying,
Implying that the finite might achieve beyond the wise,
Cries from Hera of the guile, vigilant of those smitten,
Hidden by sly Bosporus, the ox was underlying.

Relying on Prometheus to direct the maiden,
An eminent one plants a fruitful seed, a worthy deed,
His creed rebuked by his successes, nay, heed Heracles,
Glories much greater than Prometheus or any men.

When legends of compassion are tethered to man's
essence,
Vigilance will unchain mankind from the gods' insolence.

Dishonored Prometheus cannot rightly be called a sonnet,
and probably falls into a free-style verse; though I enjoyed the
challenge of keeping each line at fourteen syllables and attempting to have the end of one line rhyme or slant rhyme
with the beginning of the next. I wrote this when I was barely
20-years-old and had a great idea, or so I thought, and decided
I would try my hand at it. It became a lofty exercise in futility,
but I still wanted to share it in this collection. The story of
Prometheus was always a favorite from Greek mythology. As
you may take from this poem, I respect the man who stands
against any god in an attempt to help his brethren suffer less,
no matter the punishment.

Joshua Robertson

Lady Red

Once upon a time, a small, darling girl lived on the edge of a forest that had as many trees as the sky had stars. She was loved by all who looked upon her, yet it was her old granny who loved her most of all. So smitten, old granny was, that she made her a hood of red samite, a rich fabric unlike most. It fit her granddaughter so well that she would wear nothing else on her head, and the people called her Lady Red.

Said her mother to Lady Red, "Go see your old granny this autumn eve, and bring her this slice of cake and a bottle of wine. She has been ill and weak and these will refresh her. Behave yourself on the journey through the wood and do not venture too far from the path. Walk prettily as you stroll on the road, otherwise you might fall and break the bottle, and then poor granny will have nothing to save her from her sickness. Do not peep when you come into her room and do not forget to say 'good-day'."

Lady Red swore with her hand upon her mother's. "I will do as you say." She gathered up a basket with the cake and wine and ventured well away from her home.

But her old granny lived far out in the forest, an hour or more from the village, and Lady Red's promise slipped her mind as she walked.

Midway through the journey, as you might imagine, she came upon a wolf. Lady Red was like the harvest moon and the wolf, the night sky. She did not know what a wicked beast he was and was not afraid of him.

"May the day bring you blessings, Lady Red," said he.

"And to you be blessed, wolf!" replied she.

The wolf sulked through the trees. "Where is it you travel to so early, Lady Red?"

"To Granny's house."

"And what is it you carry, tucked under your mantle so carefully?"

Said Lady Red, with a tilt of her head, "Cake and wine. Yesterday, my mother prepared it for my old granny must have a good meal to strengthen herself and be well."

"Where does your granny live, Lady Red?"

"A good quarter of an hour's walk yet further in the forest, under yon three large oaks. Her house is solid among them; for years, it has stood. If you have reached the nut-trees then too far you have walked."

The wolf then thought within himself, *The darling girl would be a tasty treat. Surely, she would savor my hunger better than an old woman. But if played cleverly, I may catch both and be full til winter.*

By and by, the wolf schemed while walking by Lady Red's side.

Then said he, "Lady Red! Just look here at this patch of flowers we are passing! Are they not pretty? Why don't you pause and take a gander? They will be gone soon with winter coming. Do you not hear how delightful the birds are singing? You and I are walking along and how dull you seem, and yet see how cheerful it is in this forest!"

Lady Red lifted her eyes and, true enough, the sun's rays glistened against the tops of trees where birds sang, and all around them, every place was full of flowers.

"My granny will be cheered up if I brought her a sweet-smelling nosegay," admitted she. "And it is still so early in the day. I will have plenty of time to collect the prettiest flowers the forest has to offer."

The wolf shooed her onward as she went skipping off the path into the forest. She plucked a delicate one before seeing another pretty one further off, and then fancied even another. Deeper and deeper, she ran into the forest.

The wolf, however, went by the straight road to old granny's beneath the oak trees.

He knocked at the door and replied to the old granny's question of "Who's there?"

"Lady Red, who has brought cake and wine. Let me in!"

"Press the latch, dear child," cried granny, "for I am so weak that I cannot stand."

The wolf pressed the latch, walked in, and went straight to the granny's bed where he ate her up in a single bite. A full meal she was, ever so tasty, filling his belly nearly full. He then took her clothes, dressed himself in them, put her cap on his head, drew the curtains of the four-post bed, and lay down in her bed to wait for dessert.

In the meantime, Lady Red ran after flowers until she could not carry anymore. She had a fine bouquet that smelled as sweet as springtime rain. She thought of her granny and found her way back to the road.

The door stood wide open when she arrived, which seemed strange. And when she entered the room, things were even more peculiar to her. The day had already been so strange after meeting the wolf on the road. She usually felt glad in visiting her old granny, but nothing in the house seemed quite right.

She creeped to Granny's bedside and said she, "Goodday," but received no answer.

Thinking Granny was sleeping, she drew back the curtains to reveal the bed and the figure of her granny upon it. There lay Granny with her cap drawn down to her eyes and looking incredibly queer.

"Ah, Granny! Heard you were ill, I did, but why have you such long ears?"

"The better to hear you, my child."

"Ah, Granny! Heard you were ill, I did, but why have you such big eyes?"

"The better to see you, my child."

"Ah, Granny! Heard you were ill, I did, but why do you have such large hands?"

"The better to take hold of you, my child."

"Ah, Granny! Heard you were ill, I did, but why do you have such a mouth so terribly wide?"

"The better to eat you up!"

And therewith, the wolf sprang out of bed at once on poor Lady Red and ate her up.

With his appetite satisfied, the wolf lay down again in the bed and began to snore tremendously while darkness set over the forest. The clouds lay a blanket over the stars and the harvest moon so nothing could be seen in the pitch.

Alas, eventually a huntsman, the archer of the heavens, came past the granny's home with a glowing lantern in his hand. Heavy was his heart, seeing that the harvest moon was hidden that night. It had been swallowed whole, devoured by the shadowed beast of the eve. Though his thoughts wandered and he thought, *How can an old woman snore like that? I'll just have a look to see what it is.*

He went into the home and investigated the bed. To his surprise, there lay the wolf, no longer wearing the clothes or cap, nor did he have the curtains drawn.

"Found you now, I did, old rascal!" said the huntsman. "I've been looking for you." He was going to take aim with his bow when he contemplated out loud. "Perhaps, this beast has only swallowed Granny and I could save her still."

He lay down his bow and reached for his knife to cut open the sleeping wolf. But he did not know he spoke too loudly and the wolf's snoring had ceased.

To his surprise, the wolf had raised its long ears, opened its big eyes, reached out with its large hands, and snapped forward with its wide mouth. And, like that, the hunter joined the granny and Lady Red into the wolf's maw, providing him a well-satisfied tummy for the rest of winter.

During those cold months, while the wolf sat warm and plumply full in the old granny's house, it wondered who next would go off the road into the forest, even when their mother forbade it.

Gone Astray

A whispered song whistles
With a touch of a curse
Singing of hidden dreams
Written and undefined
Like a skald's song
Without the last verse
Leaves an observant path
Broken and unaligned

Joshua Robertson

Rebelling For Change

Mayhem and misery is a dream,
That this world will need to allow,
For an acceptable change to seam,
Into the heart of what is sowed.
It will only come of chaos,
On a level that is uncontrolled,
By the government or societal sauce,
That drowns the people tenfold.
A new order shoved down our throats
Is it an assertive feat that needs coaxed?
With a blazing fire and a sturdy rope,
Or can we change without being choked?

Joshua Robertson

The Prince's Parish

Chapter I

The dice dropped from Edgar's wobbly hand. His fingers trembled as if buried in midwinter snow. He swallowed a mouthful of stale air and paused. Gambling in a church was going to send the lot of them straight to perdition. His eyes widened as the dotted cubes smacked against the shoddy table-top, recoiled, and settled.

"Ginger! Three fives and a four," Morgain exclaimed. "You won. I cannot believe you actually won, Wallace." He shook his shaggy head, grinning as wide as his cheeks would allow. "I guess that's game. Ten pence apiece. Pay out, boys." Morgain slapped down his coins as an example to the rest.

"B-b-beginner's luck," Pip remarked, mirroring Morgain's smile. The bright-faced chap pulled the pence from the pouch at his waist. The lad seemed to be in good spirits.

Thomas, on the other hand, pouted from across the table. His curly, black hair hung over him like a nasty storm cloud. Thomas's face reddened all the way to his ears. Edgar did not think the table between them was strong enough to hold the lad back.

Thomas's voice cracked, marking his transition to manhood. "The whelp cheated. No one rolls three fives on their first game. Say, I have been playing Hammy for two years and never rolled three fives."

Pip clutched onto his pouch, pulling his lanky arms back to his sides like his money might be snagged from him at any moment. He nodded his head at Thomas, his white teeth disappearing behind his oversized lips. "Um, yeah, ch-ch-cheated. He must've."

Their bellyaching parroted back and forth in hushed whispers over the tattered table with Thomas complaining and Pip reiterating the statement almost word for word. Edgar was speechless, unsure of how to respond to the accusations. He felt his legs start shaking under the table. He did his best to hold them still before they started bouncing.

Morgain picked up on his discomfort and shushed the cacophony of the two disgruntled boys. "C'mon, don't be sore. You boys haven't even been here a day and you're at each other's throats. Listen, Edgar didn't cheat. He came here to be a curate of the parish like you. Only sinners cheat. Tell them, Wallace."

Edgar blinked. He had not let his eyes close since the dice hit the table. He was too afraid to say it out loud, but he was certain lightning would strike him dead for playing Hammy. The boys back home used to play it down by the watering hole when the adults were away, but he never ventured too close. His grandfather would have had his hide for risking hard-earned coins at the fate of dice.

He noticed that Morgain was nodding his head with encouragement. The older chap was almost a man, looking at him much like an older brother might. Edgar wanted to say something slick or wise but he was not quick like the others. He was the grandson of a sheepherder sent to become a curate. His childhood was spent roaming green fields and watching for wolves, not exchanging words with boisterous boys in a basement.

His mouth was dry. Footsteps resounded from the parish above them, giving Edgar a few more seconds. Minister Brus was moving around in the church, likely thinking that they were all asleep.

"Go ahead," Thomas poked. "Tell me you weren't cheating. I dare you."

"Yeah," Pip echoed, "g-g-go ahead."

His grandfather had told him it would be a good thing to serve at the Prince's Parish. This place was supposed to be safe from evil men, honoring Prince Arterbury, who ruled while the King was away at war in the Midlands. Yet, after only half a day, Edgar was gambling and picking fights with the other boys.

Edgar meekly grunted in the sound of a single word. It sounded more like a squeal. "Yeah."

"Ginger! What's wrong with you, Edgar?" Morgain asked. "You just won a month's wage fair and square. Tell 'em you weren't cheating and be done with it."

Edgar rubbed his hands against the wool that itched against his bare skin. It was not made as fine as it should have been. He was not sure why he had to trade his old clothes for this scratchy robe. "You guys can keep your pence. I didn't mean to win. Really."

"What?" Thomas snorted. "You expect us to believe you weren't trying to—" Thomas lifted his hand, palm facing the ceiling, finding a loss for words. When none filled the space, he said, "The boy is a lout. He must be plumb out of his mind. A dummy, this one."

Pip wrinkled his nose with amusement. "A d-d-dummy."

"I am not!" Edgar gushed, cheeks warming. He was certain that his ears were bright red, too, even in the dim light of the burning wax. His grandfather always said that he blushed like a girl when he was angry.

"C'mon, you two. Let him alone and pay out already. Never seen such ruckus over a boy winning fair and square in all my life," Morgain sniggered.

The throaty voice behind them nearly made Edgar jump from his chair. "Winning at what, did you say?"

"Minister Brus!" Thomas shouted, dark curls bobbing. He scooted back from the table as though it were a roaring fire about to burn his hands.

"M-m-minster Brus, he was just—"

"Pip, lying is as equal an abomination to any other sin. The common man may ask forgiveness, but a man of the church would have his tongue cut out. It would be my duty to see it done under the law. Prince Arterbury is quite particular about these matters." Minister Brus looked on Pip with sorrow, his eyes pleading to keep him from seeing the task done. His ruffled eyebrows were fuddled, arched and quivering upon his wrinkled forehead. His old lips smacked, pressing his graying stubble to his shaggy mustache.

Minister Brus could have been as old as the church. Edgar had met him when arriving that morning, but it was only now that he truly noticed the age of the old man.

Pip second guessed himself, sitting straighter, mouth gawking. "H-h-he was gambling. We all were gambling."

Thomas socked Pip in the shoulder. "Say, we didn't mean nothing by it, Minister Brus."

"I see," the Minister said, folding his hands in front of him. "Gambling is punishable in the same way as stealing, I'm afraid."

Edgar gulped, nearly afraid to ask, "And, how is that, Minister Brus?"

"Lashings and severed limbs." He replied. His voice was desolate, heart-breaking.

"L-l-lashings?"

"Yes, Pip. With the cat-o-nine-tails—in the courtyard—for all to bear witness." Minister Brus was as solemn as any priest would be when giving his sermon from the pulpit. "The Prince," he paused to look to the distance, as though he could see the castle through the parish walls, a short distance away, "will frequently deliver the thrashing himself. The man is a warlord, you know, like his brother. Strong and steadfast. One lashing will tear through to the spine."

Pip squeaked, "How many?"

"Ten." Minister Brus was quick to answer. "More if you flinch."

Edgar's heart sank, caring little about the lashings, but worrying more about the latter punishment. "You will really cut off our hands?"

Minister Brus guffawed, unable to keep the joke going any longer, spraying droplets of saliva from between the edges of his sagging mouth. He gripped his belly and threw his head back with such force he could have snapped his own neck.

Morgain, who had been quietly stifling his own laughter, chortled, "You will have these younglings wetting the bed like infants talking like that, Minister. You are supposed to be the parish priest, not a trickster."

Edgar heaved a sigh.

Minister swatted his hand in the air good-naturedly. "I am a lot of things with timeworn being the topmost. I, too, need moments of jollity when serving in this monstrosity—erm—monastery. Now, place your bets and fetch me a chair. The night is still young."

Chapter II

Edgar shielded his eyes from the morning sun. The golden ball hovered just above the easternmost tower of Arterbury Castle. The fire that burned nearby in the courtyard was stifling with white smoke churning towards the sky. Sweat dripped from his brow already and the rooster had barely crowed.

"Let's hurry it up," Thomas snorted, trekking by him with a hacked limb thrown over his shoulder. The boy seemed to be as strong as a grown man. "Morgain will be back in a bit to check on our work and we aren't even halfway done."

Pip sniffed. His arms were as tense as barbed wire, dragging a smaller branch at a snail's pace toward the burn pit. "I-I-I'm trying."

"I don't think anyone has picked up this yard in half a century." Edgar gulped a mouthful of the spring morning, clutching a log under his arms awkwardly. He waddled towards the pile of burning brush where Thomas had already dropped his load and was turning back to find more wood.

"You fell asleep a good three hours before the rest of us, Edgar, and you are moving the slowest. Even Minister Brus was up before you. Better pick it up, or I am going to think those stories about sheep farmers sleeping all day are true."

"This is a lot heavier," Edgar huffed, "than what you were carrying."

"That's a laugh!" Thomas hooted, raising his arms and flexing for show. "My branch was twice as long."

"And needle thin," Edgar muttered.

Thomas threw down his arms and marched over to block Edgar, "What was that, boy?"

Edgar lifted his eyes, unable to stand straight because of the weight of the log. Thomas's face was nearly as red as it had been the night before. The lad was maybe a smidgeon older that Edgar, but even while stooped, Edgar could look straight into his enraged eyes. Thomas was as livid as a cat in gunnysack.

"N-n-needle thin," Pip repeated. He froze when Thomas cranked his head around and glowered. "Ah, b-b-but it was a b-b-bit b-b-bigger than a needle." He shuffled his feet to try to get his branch closer to the flames.

"Damn straight." Thomas puffed up his chest, face red as the cherries Edgar used to pick from the tree outside his grandfather's house.

Edgar swallowed. The boy was swearing! Edgar was not sure how to respond or if he should respond at all. The hefty kid did not budge, squinting back like a half-deranged hog searching for its slop. Edgar tried to ease the tension, "Why—"

"You don't think I can lift that?" he interrupted, challenging.

Edgar had never met a kid so bent on causing conflict. Already, his muscles were starting to shake from the weight of the log. "Let's just get done, like you said," Edgar finally managed to blurt out.

"Say, you think I'm weak!"

Edgar knew Thomas was not really asking him a question. The lad's eyes were glassed over with emotion. Edgar had seen the same look and heard the same tone from his grandfather, like the time when he had forgotten to latch the gate and half a dozen sheep had gone missing. The difference was that his grandfather had a switch to act out his anger; Thomas only had his bouncing, black curls.

"Give me that," Thomas scoffed, yanking the wood from his fingers. Edgar flinched as small splinters pierced his hands. "This is not that heavy, you dummy." With a grunt, Thomas reeled sideways and threw the log toward the red-hot flames.

Edgar yelled in dismay, dread filling his chest. In horror, he ogled at the log that wheeled towards the pit—and Pip. Next to him, Thomas's face transformed from smug to shock to panic, while his throat became gagged by his own half-hearted bawl.

Unaware, Pip let loose his branch into the licking flames as the log smashed into the middle of his back. The boy flailed his gangly arms and lurched forward, rocking on his toes only to plunge forward into the piping hot fire.

Pip's squeal started before he landed in the embers and twisted into a blood-curdling shriek as the inferno splashed around his ragged robes and youthful flesh. The wool of his clothing caught flame straightaway. The cries intensified, mixed with whimpers and wails, as poor Pip writhed, flailing and rolling, looking for something to grab that was not burning.

His skin was melting from muscle. Black and bloodied.

"No!" Edgar cried, rushing for Pip.

"Goddammit!" Thomas screeched, sprawling to the edge of the pit. "I am going to be in trouble now."

Edgar rotated to Thomas to look away from the burning boy. There was no way to pull him free without getting burnt himself.

"Water," Edgar said. "We need to find water."

No more had he said the words that a bucket full of water splashed into the pit behind him, sending up ash and smoke, eliciting a fettered outcry from Pip as it hit his flesh. Another wave of water crashed into the woodpile causing a similar effect.

The fire still burned.

"Get more water!" Morgain slammed the bucket into Edgar's chest, pushing him towards the parish. Edgar grunted, stumbling back to do as he was asked. Minister Brus was waving his arms and shouting frantically at Thomas.

The boy only gaped at Pip.

Edgar reached out to take the bucket from Minister Brus and pulled at Thomas. The other boy did not react; his feet didn't cooperate. Instead, his eyes locked on Pip, unmoving.

"Come on!" Edgar shouted at Thomas.

"Let it be," Minister Brus blubbered, giving up and falling to his knees. "The boy is dead."

Chapter III

"I have sent a pigeon to the Prince to inform him of the situation," Minister Brus said, walking with difficulty toward the chair behind his desk. His eyes were still irritated, swollen from crying. "I have sent another to Pip's family. I expect they will be here within a couple days to collect his remains."

The quarters of the priest were silent in response. Morgain stood hunched near the window, staring out at the smoldering smoke that had begun to thin out. One hand was glued to his hip, and the other raking through his hair. The older boy did not seem to have the strength to look at Edgar or Thomas.

Edgar's jaw quivered. He was certain that he was the worst boy to ever walk into the Prince's Parish. He had gambled, squabbled, and watched a boy die, all within a day's time.

Thomas, sitting next to him in an identical wooden chair, had his arms crossed. The boy's eyebrows were angled in such a way that they could nearly fill the space between his eyes. His lips were pressed outward, nostrils flaring. His gaze was fixed on Minister Brus like the holy man was the devil himself.

Edgar looked away as chills started to creep up his arms and neck. He knew that he had done terrible things, but Thomas had bad blood. The boy was as unwavering in his wrath as he was with his breath.

"Pip was stupid," Thomas groused between clenched teeth. "The stuttering dummy knew we were working and hovered over the fire like a…a half-brained lout!"

"Thomas!" Minister Brus rocked back in his chair, hands pressed to the table. "That is no way to speak. Where is your compassion? The boy was barely here a day and has died…." The Minister turned his head away, shaking it as though he were trying to make sense of what had happened. He noticeably swallowed and folded his shaking hands. "It was a misfortunate incident but we should not be looking for blame."

Thomas squirmed under the harsh tone of the priest.

"It was an accident," Edgar uttered.

"Of course," Minister Brus dipped his head. "The Prince will come and see that the parish is exonerated, and that the family's heartache is lessened…whatever can be done."

Thomas balled his fists in his lap, face inflamed as ever, all the way to his ears. "Say, it was an accident. I don't see why you had to go and tell the Prince. You are trying to get me in trouble. He may hang me or worse."

Minister Brus inhaled, blinking several times before blowing out. "No, no. I am not trying to do anything, especially have any of you hanged. You are but a boy, Thomas. I am certain that the Prince will forgive this mishap. After all, it was an accident."

His gentle, widened eyes searched Thomas and Edgar.

"It truly was," Edgar said.

"We best be sure before the Priest comes," Morgain rattled from the window. It was likely the first time he had said a word since they had come inside. "We need to know what happened exactly. Have 'em tell us their story, word for word."

Edgar opened his mouth to explain but was cut off by Morgain.

"Separately."

Minister Brus looked to Morgain and after a moment, nodded. "Indeed. It would be wise to have the details before the Prince arrives. I will take Thomas to the basement, and you can speak to Edgar up here in my office. When we are done, we can reconvene and look for any inconsistencies in the story."

Edgar could feel Thomas's eyes burning into him. He kept his eyes straight forward, refusing to look at the boy and his dark curls.

"Come with me, Thomas." The Minister stood up from his chair, the wood scraping against the flooring, and headed for the door. The boy stood nonchalantly and made his way toward the door, but not before whispering in Edgar's ear.

"Say this is my fault and you're next."

Edgar trembled. His eyes darted to Morgain, gazing out the window, and Minister Brus, halfway out the door. Neither had heard the threat.

Would Thomas really kill him, too?

The door clicked shut, leaving Edgar alone with Morgain. The older man, who had acted like a brother yesterday, had lost the tenderness shown from the night before.

His voice was broken, distorted with agony, "Geez, Edgar. Just start from the beginning."

"I…." Edgar listened for footsteps, turning to face the door and then twisting back toward Morgain. He could not figure out why Thomas thought he would try to blame him, or anyone. It was an accident. "There is not much to say. We were moving wood like we were told, cleaning up the yard and all."

"C'mon. Keep going." A twinge of kindness surfaced on Morgain's face, his cheekbones relaxing.

Edgar settled into his chair a bit, trying to calm down. Morgain was not blaming him for Pip's death. "Is the Prince going to question us, too?"

"I don't know." Morgain cracked his knuckles. "Please, tell me what happened."

"Okay." Edgar gulped. He had to tell the truth, no matter what Thomas threatened. He would not be adding lying to his list of unforgivable sins. "I was carrying a piece of wood to put in the fire pit. Thomas came and took it out of my hands and threw it, without looking, and accidently knocked him in."

"Who?"

Edgar shifted in his chair, "Pip. He accidently knocked Pip in the fire." The study blurred as tears started to fill his eyes and stream down his cheeks. It was instant, like water from a natural spring, choking him up. "I mean we ran to the fire as soon as it happened, but there was no way to pull him—to pull Pip—out, you see? It was too hot. The flames were way too high! And Pip could not get out either. He was screaming and crying…."

"Ginger!" Morgain stood up, suddenly regretting his suggestion. He, too, had water dripping down his face. "I'm sorry, Edgar. It might be too soon to talk about this. It's okay."

"It's really not." Edgar shook his head, burying his face into his hands. "It's terrible!"

Morgain's hand touched his shoulder.

Before the older boy could say something comforting, a crash and clatter sounded from beyond the door.

"What?" Morgain jerked towards the door, rushing out. Edgar strained to follow, his legs feeling as heavy as the logs he had been carrying. Morgain pulled ahead rushing toward the basement at the opposite end of the church.

"Ginger! What happened?" He could hear Morgain shouting.

Thomas's voice was as waterless as a dried-out riverbed. "Minister Brus slipped and fell down the stairs. I think the old cod broke his neck."

Chapter IV

Morgain and Prince Arterbury had been within Minister Brus's quarters for the past two hours. The door had not opened for any reason. The two had not come out for drinks or even leg-stretching since they had entered the study. The Prince had arrived in a carriage, defended by more men with swords and crossbows than Edgar had ever seen in his life. The guards had stayed outside the parish, disallowed from bringing weapons inside the holy church.

Edgar twiddled his thumbs, his legs shaking as he sat in the pew in front of the pulpit. The parish priest's office was only a handful of feet away. Edgar strained, as he had for the last couple hours, trying to hear what was being said. Nothing.

"What did you tell Morgain?" Thomas scooted closer to him on the long seat, hissing between his pursed lips. "You didn't say it was my fault, did you?"

"No," Edgar whispered. Even with a single word, his voice was clearly shaky. He glanced at the sturdy kid out of his peripheral, unsure of what to expect. He had threatened him right before Minister Brus had died, but why?

Thomas was calm, with the composure as sheep sleeping in the pasture.

Edgar asked, "Aren't you upset?"

"About what?" he asked, clearing his throat.

Edgar wiped his eyes, focusing on the layered wool that hung over his knees. "Pip. Minister Brus. They are dead, Thomas."

"So?"

Edgar could not believe his ears. "What does that mean? Don't you think it is horrible that there have been two deaths since we have arrived here? Doesn't that seem odd? I cannot help but wonder if we are being punished for something." Edgar kept his eyes off the dais where the priest would usually give his sermons. He was sure there was a religious idol or statue somewhere that would be overlooking him, judging him.

"Are you a dummy, really?" Thomas said wryly from the corner of his mouth. "Say, you think that a god is trying to chastise us for wanting to be curates?" He chortled in his throat. "You act like you have never lost anyone before or ever seen anyone die."

Edgar swallowed. "I have, too. My parents both died when I was around five. They had the sickness, and I was sent to live with my grandfather. But it isn't natural—"

"Ha! It is about as natural as it gets. We all die. It's really the whole point of life."

"I was saying it isn't natural for so many to happen at once." Edgar said, scowling from being interrupted. "I wonder what is going to happen now. The Prince's Parish doesn't have a parish priest."

"Who cares?" Thomas snorted. "I didn't want to come here anyway. My pa said it was better to serve the church than be strung up in the stockades.

"The stockades? For what?"

Thomas ignored the question. "Besides, I don't think it will be the last one."

"What?" Edgar spun on his haunches. The boy had his eyebrows angled once more with the dark curls casting a shadow over his eyes. Thomas looked more menacing than a wolf that Edgar might face in the field while protecting his grandfather's flock. "What do you mean by that?"

Thomas shrugged, facing the door to the study. "Just saying that Morgain isn't the most pleasant fellow. I wouldn't be surprised if he fell down a flight of stairs, too, shouting 'Ginger!' the whole way down."

"That is not funny! That is not something to be joked about."

"I'm guessing there is a better chance of breaking your neck if you are given a little push, is all." Thomas winked.

Edgar's worst fears were becoming a reality. He nearly felt unsafe uttering the words, "You pushed Minister Brus down the stairs?"

Thomas scooted closer to Edgar like he was springing from a trap. Edgar shifted, moving further away from the boy. His heart was racing. Thomas continued to advance across the wood bench with a strange expression on his face, contorted with delight. When Edgar smacked into the railing at the edge of the pew, he tried to move further but was trapped by Thomas, who had his eyes locked onto him with a haunting glimmer of excitement.

His voice was raspy, still at a murmur, "Did you see Pip's eyes fade out when he died? It was hard to see with the flames and the bastard thrashing about, but it was…like magic. Yes, so unbelievably magical! Say, if you looked close enough, you could see the light flee from his body with his last breath. It was like it had somewhere else to go." Thomas grinned. "I wonder where it went."

Edgar held his own breath. He had never been so afraid. He struggled to hold back tears.

"Minister Brus died so much quicker. I mean, don't get me wrong. I rushed down the stairs as fast as I could. I grabbed his head and lopped it sideways to catch sight of the same thing. But I was too late. His neck snapped and—well, that was it. No breathing. No heartbeat. No light. I wonder if folks have to die really slow to watch the light disappear."

"You killed…him."

Thomas ignored Edgar, "I bet if we kill Morgain slow, we could learn more about what happens to that light behind the eyes. Say, we could tie him up. Cut him and watch the blood drain away drop by drop. We would have to take our time. Be deliberate. We cannot be hurried, not like with Pip or the Minister."

Edgar's breath funneled out through his lips. He wanted to cry, to puke, to scream. He could barely speak. "You really killed them."

"Mm," Thomas shifted his eyes toward the study. "Don't worry. I'll let you play with me next time. Just don't spoil the surprise." He tapped Edgar on the knee. "I would hate to kill you, too. Though that would be something, wouldn't it? Say, it is really something! Nothing like with mice and kittens."

Edgar's stomach bubbled. He pressed his lips together to keep himself from blowing chunks.

The study door creaked open and Morgain walked out. His shaggy hair clung to his ears, nearly to his sagging shoulders. There was no smile on his face, not like there had been yesterday when they were gambling in the basement. The man was shattered. Edgar could only picture him with blood dripping slowly from his body.

Thomas scooted to the side, squaring off on the seat as though nothing had happened. Edgar gripped his knees; they were shaking beyond his control.

"The Prince has declared both deaths an unfortunate accident. He has," Morgain cleared his throat, "appointed me as the Parish Priest in the absence of the Minister."

"What should we do?" Thomas said, holding back a grimace. "Can we go home?"

Morgain shook his head, caught up in his own misery. "No, we have our duty as the holy men of this church. We will continue to care for the estate. Though, I think it is best we take the day for mourning and rest. We will speak again in the morning."

Chapter V

Edgar's eyes burned, bloodshot and dry. He closed his eyelids, a wave of sleepiness washing over him, coaxing him to lay down on the cot.

He jerked, almost falling out of the bed. His head was heavy, and his body was sore from lifting the logs, but he could not sleep. Edgar was certain that the moment that his eyes shut, Thomas would wake up and gut him. He bit his inner lip until he tasted blood.

"Ow." He mumbled, holding the side of his face.

A stammering grunt bounced off the basement's stone wall on the other side of the room. He froze in his cross-legged position. It reminded him of Pip stuttering.

Edgar peered through the darkness that engulfed the basement. He could not see past his nose. Nothing stirred. He could only hear the reverberation of the boy across the room. It seemed that Thomas was still sleeping, snoring.

At snail's pace, Edgar inched out of the cot, balancing his weight to reduce any creaking or squeaking. His feet pressed against the chilled, gritty stone floor. Lifting his hands, he steadied his footing and stepped forward into the pitch. After two steps, his knee hit something hard.

A chair. He was near the table in the center of the room, where he had sat and gambled only yesterday evening. That meant he was only a few feet from the staircase that led upstairs. The plan was simple. If he could make it up the stairs and find a way to block the door, then he could tell Morgain about Thomas. Morgain was nearly a man and was now the parish priest. He would know what to do.

Edgar took another step, his foot banging into the table. The sound echoed and the snoring stopped. He held his breath.

"What are you doing, you dummy?" Thomas's voice was clear. He did not sound as though he had been sleeping at all.

Edgar suppressed a whimper. "Going to the bathroom."

A light flashed as Thomas lit a candle near his cot. A small glow flooded the basement, illuminating the boy's dark curls and cold gaze. "In the dark?"

"Y-y-yes." Edgar's chin trembled. He could not stand to look at Thomas. His eyes fell to the tabletop where the dice were still lying from the previous night. His three fives and the four were still face up. The dark dots were reflected by the pale glow of the candlelight.

"Say," Thomas stood up, "why don't I go with you?" He held the candle outright in front of him, swishing it back and forth in the air impishly. "It can be dangerous walking about in the dark all by yourself."

Edgar said, "Thanks, Thomas. I don't have to go anymore. I am just going to go back to bed. Goodnight."

Thomas tilted his chin, "Oh, c'mon, you dummy. You have me out of bed. We might as well have some fun while we are awake. You think Morgain is awake?"

"I...I don't know." Edgar said, settling back on his heels. He tried to be brave, but his nerves were rattled. "I will see you in the morning."

"I see." Thomas clicked his tongue on the roof of his mouth a few times, his hands shifting against his body, a silhouette against the light. "Say, I don't think you were going to the bathroom at all. In fact, I wonder if you were aiming to go tell Morgain what we had talked about earlier."

Edgar shuddered, his breath rushing from his nostrils.

"You was!" Thomas inferred, eyebrows slanting. Even in the dark, Edgar could see the redness in his cheeks. "I cannot have that." The dark-curled boy moved towards Edgar and put the candle down on the table.

"What are you doing?"

Thomas did not say a word. He balled up his fist and took another step.

"Stay back!" Edgar shouted.

"None of that now," Thomas shushed.

Edgar did not know how the chair had come into his hands, but he swooped it upwards and clocked Thomas in the upper body. Blood oozed from the shorter boy's lip on impact, causing him to grab his mouth and stumble back. He sneered, seeing his own blood.

"You half-brained lout! Look at what you did," Thomas bellowed.

He rested the chair on the ground.

"I'll get you for this!" Thomas rumbled with fury and stormed forward again. His eyes were dusky, shadowed by his curls. He reached to pull the chair from Edgar's grasp.

Edgar cried out, as he imagined a fighter might on a distant battlefield and yanked the chair back toward him before swinging it forward with all his strength. Over and over again. It struck Thomas in the nose, chin, and chest. Thomas's high-pitched scream rebounded off the walls. It sounded like a sheep bleating while being ripped apart by a pack of wolves. Edgar did not stop.

This was life or death.

Thomas fell to the ground, his legs crumbling underneath him with his arms raised to protect himself. Edgar's guttural roar was unlike any sound he had ever heard come from his own throat. He brought the chair down time after time, again and again, against the devilish child.

The boy was a murderer.

At some point, Thomas brought his head up to crawl away, and the chair broke when hitting his skull. Thomas collapsed into a motionless heap. The screams of his enemy were reduced to whimpers, then silence.

Edgar did not stop.

Crimson liquid gushed and flooded across the floor. Blood oozed. He ignored the warmness against his bare toes.

"Stop! Edgar!" Morgain's voice pleaded from the darkness. "Ginger!" Strong hands wrapped around him, pulling him away. He swung the chair mercilessly, assuring that the murderer was dead.

In the feeble ruddiness of the flame, Edgar clung to Morgain. "I had to stop him. He killed Pip. He killed Minister Brus. He was going to kill you, too!" He affixed his gaze to Thomas's dastardly eyes, emptily staring back at him. The light within faded away…like magic.

Six Feet Down

Bury me beneath,
The wooden lid has been sealed
I am still alive.

Hear my weakened cry
Beyond the coffin, I lie,
My breath is shallow.

Dirt rains over me,
Suffering suffocation.
Dirt rains over me.

Alone with the worms,
My brains are for the maggots,
I am forgotten.

Six Feet Down was written with the haiku in mind, which are typically three lines with seventeen syllables, I wanted to build on the simplicity and intensity of several haikus strung together with a singular focus.

Joshua Robertson

The Burden of Memories

Ashes flutter down from above,
spinning in the currents of dust,
like lone butterflies with wings trussed.
Lying here beneath the debris,
Each remnant leads to injury,
No memory will I soon trust,
Ashes flutter down.

Thus did I live; thus did I love,
The weight on my mind is unjust,
Heavy soot binds me in disgust,
Can't say what I was thinking of,
Ashes flutter down.

The Burden of Memories was written in the rondeau prime poetry style. The poem was a reflection on the onslaught of thoughts that riddle our minds and keep us from moving forward in our journey in life. In my youth, I struggled to be mindful of the present moment and frequently would feel encumbered by my past.

Joshua Robertson

A Twist of Fate

Radan half-listened to the tune of crackling flames splitting wood in his open fireplace. While sleep tugged at his eyelids, he would continue working for hours. Entwining his quill pen through his long fingers, he studied the leather-bound ledger spread out over his desk. A courier from the ziggurat, Tipol, had delivered the monthly register two days ago. Radan wished he had made the time to rewrite the numbers yesterday or even early this morning. He wanted nothing more than to sip spiced wine and find his bed.

"Master Radan." His broad-shouldered servant suddenly appeared in the open doorway of the study. Vid's speech was broken as though he were fighting to speak a foreign language. "A message has come."

Pulling the wide sleeves of his modest robe up over his elbows, Radan momentarily ignored the bumbling brute. He dipped the pen into the ink jar and began to copy the first set of numbers. He was familiar with the scribbled figures running up and down each column, detailing the tens of thousands of shekels collected for funerary rites from Stemir patrons living throughout Barava.

As usual, he would spend as much time as needed transcribing the document to be included in the tomes of the great library. His special assignment demanded an intellect lost to most races. Lord Nergal trusted him to deflate the recorded sums ever so slightly to hide a veritable fortune of untaxed profits.

Of course, if any neighboring city-state learned of his activities, the information would be used to incriminate Nergal in the Stemir courts. The emperor could strip Lord Nergal of his rulership over their province—it could even start a war. Radan hated to even consider the possible consequences for himself. For now, he preferred only to think of the coin lining his pockets. A familiar proverb claimed *neither fortunes nor flowers last forever*, but for Radan, life without fortune was fruitless.

A little risk meant nothing when compared to a life of luxury.

"Master Radan?" Vid's deep tone echoed off the shelves.

"I heard you the first time." Radan elevated his eyes enough to glare at the oaf without bothering to fully lift his chin. Vid was known as a Gourman, a common race in the world, bred to take as many punches as they could dish out. Gourman were generally considered better soldiers than servants; though when Vid came to Radan to settle an accumulated sum owed from a gambling debt, he surrendered many liberties, including whatever natural talents he had. In the end, Radan saw no reason to rush to grant Vid his freedom. Having Vid do odds and ends gave him more time to enjoy his riches.

Radan said harshly, "These figures are permanent registers of our province's worth. They provide a record of Lord Nergal's governance as he sees fit. Do you wish me to make a mistake? How many times must I tell you? My work is delicate."

"No," Vid answered his pretentious question a bit too slowly.

Radan snorted, taking his time to finish a full column of numbers. He then lay down his pen. "You were gone for quite some time this afternoon. What took you so long?"

"I was at the market getting the copper and lamp oil you requested." Vid cleared his throat while scratching the back of his bald head. His words flowed like molasses. "A large caravan of cavern-dwellers came into town to trade their wares. They were difficult to navigate through. They have an unusual way of finding their way under your feet."

"The rodent scum should stay in their mines," Radan muttered when Vid finally finished speaking. "Did you know their women's breasts drag on the ground?"

"I have heard stories—"

"Stories you no doubt enjoyed. I suspect you would like that sort of thing!" Radan waggled his head at Vid with disgust, glad he stopped the brute from prattling on. He added, "Do not even try to deny it. I have seen Gourman women. They are as ugly as the men."

Vid twisted his short neck and wrinkled his bulging brow. Lifting the wrapped cloth in his hand, he repeated himself, "A message has arrived for you, Master Radan."

"And what maniac would deliver anything so late? Couriers seldom run the streets after night has fallen," Radan said.

The servant lifted his shoulders.

Radan grimaced and motioned for Vid to come closer. "Bring it here, you idiot."

The lesser humanoid lumbered forward, his thick scent—akin to the blending of rotten eggs and beer—reached Radan's senses long before he actually did.

Radan rubbed the length of his conical head—a telltale sign of his superior people—which stretched almost a foot and a half above his eyes, and he visibly gagged. His curt comment came in a huff as Vid extended his meaty hand to reveal a bundle of black cloth. "How many times must I tell you? My home must remain as civilized a place as our greater province. You must wash regularly. No guest would visit knowing you traipse through my hallways."

"Exalted One," Vid said with reluctance, "bathing is not a normal thing. You must understand that my wives would reject me if I were to smell like your fancy oils and perfumes."

"Your fat, dirty wives, you mean?" Radan scoffed. "What do you care what they think? You have not seen them in months."

"I would be glad to return soon." Vid clumsily dipped his head with his arm still outstretched.

Radan eyeballed the brute with wonder, motioning with his fingers. "I am sure you would. Yet your days of service are far from over, even though you reek of sweat and urine." He frowned. "Give me the package."

Vid clamped his lips shut like a good servant, keeping his thoughts from escaping his slave tongue. At least he knew when to keep quiet. Although Radan had the ability to take the parcel without effort, he was pleased to see Vid take an unnecessary step forward to set the bundle on his desk.

Radan smiled to himself and examined the package.

The thick linen was folded into a square with something distinctly bulging from the center. No markings existed, nor did Radan find a note. Only a thin cord could be seen, securely holding the fabric in place with a solidified knot in the center. His smile faded as he squinted at the strange bundle. He often received pamphlets and letters, but never anything so bulky. Without acknowledging Vid, who noisily breathed on the opposite side of the desk, Radan untied the cord.

His stomach immediately turned as he jerked back the final layer of linen. The sight nearly caused him to forget Vid's haunting stench altogether.

"Mercy!" Radan cried out, scooting his chair back to escape the small, severed hand resting in the folds. He stood upright, glaring at Vid, if for no other reason than to avoid looking at the pigmented appendage in front of him. "Who delivered this?"

Vid cleared his throat, darting his eyes between Radan and the freshly detached hand. "I found it on our doorstep, Exalted One. No messenger was in sight."

"You blind halfwit," Radan growled, daring to glance at it again from the corner of his eye. "Do you know what this means?"

"I believe I do, Master Radan," Vid garbled, his slow speech increasingly annoying in the present situation. "I have heard that some crime syndicates send the hand of a cavern-dweller to those marked for death. Every available cutthroat and assassin will soon start their hunt. No place is safe, not even sanctuary cities."

Radan bobbed his head, surprised that his simple servant knew anything at all. "Yes, Vid. Someone undoubtedly intends to kill someone in this residence." He gulped. "We cannot be certain the parcel was meant for me, yet I have no family living here. We—"

"You think it was sent for me, Master?" Vid strained his face in what may have been shock or terror. He looked about the study, his mouth gaping. "No other person stays in your home except you and me. I have no enemies. Oh, please! If I am meant to die, let me go see my wives and children once more. I will leave at once."

Vid waited for permission.

Radan ran his hand along his head, squinting incredulously at the beefy Gourman. "Bah! No one is scheming to kill an imbecile like you unless they are forced to cut your neck to get to mine." He rubbed his chin. "We must be certain I was the intended recipient."

"I answered a knock at the door and the package is all I found," Vid said.

Radan flared his nostrils at the simple logic. "The message must be for me, then. I must have offended or cheated some lowlife scum. Though it is more likely a rival city knows our lord has me falsifying these numbers."

He looked at the ledger, his heart quickening. He knew his work could be dangerous but never believed anyone would learn what his job truly entailed.

"Exalted—"

"It is no matter," Radan interrupted him, surveying Vid. He rubbed his elongated head again in thought. The Gourman was built for battle, and while Vid never lifted a weapon in Radan's service, he knew the brute exhibited martial prowess. Vid would defend him. He lifted his chin, wetting his lips before speaking. "You will fell whatever man or beast comes for me. Whether you stay awake this night or for a fortnight, you will guard me and my home. You might even shave a few shekels from your debt in the process. Go on and don your armor; gather your weapons."

"Master Radan, I—I will fight whatever enemy comes through the door if you demand it." Vid rumbled in his throat and sputtered. He did not budge from his spot on the floor. "Though you cannot believe I can fend off an army of assassins. Whether I kill three or three hundred, more will come. I will die."

"In exchange for my life," Radan snipped. "You should consider it an honor."

Even with his ashen skin, Radan could see Vid pale. "Yes, an honor, it would be. Yet we would still both die."

He raised his hand to shush the halfwit before he could continue his protest. While Vid was undeniably stupid in most cases, he was ultimately right in that he could not defend Radan against a steady stream of determined assassins.

Not forever, anyway.

"We must consider what we know of the secret crime syndicates," Radan said after a moment. He spun away from his desk to examine the books lining the shelves of his study. The titles of books on currency and customs, races and religions, and worlds beyond his own covered the space between the ceiling and floorboards. He was sure only a few texts were written on assassinations. He did not own a single copy.

"I have heard stories about their victims," Vid offered. He fought to speak clearly; every word seemed to steal his strength. "I heard once marked, escape is impossible. Every mercenary, guard, and even the shields of past emperors have fallen against assassins."

Radan grimaced. "I do not care about those who live and die by the sword. I am from a superior race. How many of my kind have they killed?"

"I do not know, Master Radan. They kill all kinds."

He leveled his gaze at his servant, adding a hard smile. "Either tell me something worthwhile or keep your mouth shut."

Vid scratched his head as though he were taking Radan's words seriously. "I know they arrive swiftly after the token is delivered. I would guess you do not have much time."

The smile diminished. "I believe you already said that. Thank you for reminding me." Radan adjusted the sleeves of his robe. The loose-fitting garment might protect him from watchful eyes on the streets, especially if he kept the hood pulled over his coned head. "I will go to Lord Nergal and tell him of this threat. He will make short work of any enemy of mine. For years, I have done as he instructed, and none can perform this duty as well as I."

Radan murmured more reassurances to himself, hoping the assassins had not already entered his home. The fire popped and snapped behind him while he listened for movement in the hallway beyond the study door. Outside of Vid's heavy breathing and the hissing flames, he heard little else. The silence chilled his spine. He moved to the desk, pushing the cloth and hand to the side. He then closed the ledger and tucked it under his arm.

"Vid, you will escort me to the lord's manor."

"Exalted One," Vid rustled, rubbing his hands against his thighs. "I—what if—"

Radan shouted through clenched teeth. "Spit it out! What if *what*?"

"What if Lord Nergal paid the assassins?" Vid blurted.

Radan dropped the ledger almost as quickly as he had picked it up. He could not think of an appropriate expletive to express his shock. He was dumbfounded. "Why would the lord of our province order my assassination?"

Vid flinched, lowering his voice to a whisper. His chilling words were spoken with more clarity than Radan had ever heard from Vid, as though someone else spoke through the idiot. "Maybe those in other provinces know about your work. I would think Lord Nergal would be quick to deflect the blame. He would not risk a war with his allies."

If gods ever spoke through a lesser being, Radan realized this might be that moment. He took a step back. "I am the scapegoat," he realized. "Lord Nergal wishes to silence me before I say anything of his schemes!"

"I cannot know, Master Radan…." Vid's voice trailed off.

Radan filled in the blanks; he did not need Vid to be sure of anything. He tensed his jaw, staring at the severed hand lying on his desk. The answer was sitting right in front of him. "You said the cavern-dwellers were in the market today. The assassins likely took a hand from one of them after receiving their payment from Lord Nergal. The timing is too perfect." Radan could feel the heat touching his ears. He had been betrayed. "Did you see any suspicious individuals at the market?"

Vid ruffled his brow again. "Always, my Master."

A painful lump formed in Radan's throat. He knew his question was not sensible. He took a long, low sigh. "What choice do I have? I must flee," he said. "We will gather what we can and leave the province at once."

"Where will you go that the assassins cannot find you?" Vid asked.

"There is a port to the north. We will sail across the sea," Radan said. "I will not let them have the pleasure of taking my life."

"But Master, it is forbidden to leave port without permission from Lord Nergal," Vid replied. "I once heard of a coin counter who ran. He did not make it far." Radan gripped the edge of his desk. His heart thudded louder with every word he heard. "When the assassins caught up with him, they tortured him. They flayed his skin and sawed off his legs before killing him."

"Why should I care what happened to a simpleton?" Radan shouted wildly at his servant. He made a fist and pressed it to his mouth, knowing Vid would not have an answer for him. Even if the oaf had something more to say, Radan did not want to hear it. He could not have his body dismembered and disgraced like a lesser creature. He was superior! He was in charge of his own destiny. He paced around the study, dropping his hands to clutch his body as though the act would keep him grounded. "If I cannot seek help and I cannot flee, what should I do?"

The question was more for himself than Vid. His servant said nothing.

A sour taste filled Radan's mouth.

"I cannot be shamed like this," he said.

"They will be here soon," Vid grumbled.

"I know!" Radan said, eyeing the room from the floor to the rafters. His wealth was gone. His life was over. He could not escape, but he could choose the way to reach an inevitable end. "Bring me a rope."

"Master?"

"Bring me a rope!"

Vid dipped his head shakily and shambled from the room.

Radan watched the daft Gourman leave and then returned to his desk to find a blank piece of paper and a quill. He immediately went to work, writing a detailed letter of his responsibilities in the province. He would not be silenced. He may die, but every city across these lands and beyond would know of Lord Nergal's offenses.

Something crashed outside his door in the hallway.

Radan froze, hearing only the sound of his heartbeat thrashing in his ears. His instincts urged him to shout for Vid, but his breath caught in his throat. Besides, he was too intelligent to cry out. He raked the room with his eyes, nearly expecting an assassin to jump out from the darkened corners.

What felt like a second lifetime passed, and then Vid appeared in the doorway holding a coiled rope over his shoulder.

"Have they come?" Radan hissed.

"I heard something," Vid said, shuffling forward. "But I saw nothing but shadows."

Radan sensed the sweat beads forming on his brow. He gestured for Vid to come closer. "Make me a hangman's noose and hurry. I will not be slaughtered by those savages. I will rob them of their duty and whatever payment they might receive."

Vid did not question his authority. He slung the rope from his thick shoulder, looping it and tying a slipknot on both ends.

"You will take my letter," Radan said in a whisper, folding the letter carefully. "You will deliver it to every lord who will hear it and tell them of this treachery, Vid. When you are finished, you can go see your fat wives and consider your debt repaid."

"Yes, Exalted One," Vid replied, eyeing the letter. His face was stone.

Radan carefully climbed on his desk, stood tall, and straightened his robes. He motioned to the rafters. "Throw the rope over and tie it off. And make haste, you half-wit. They are coming."

Vid did as he was instructed, making the toss in a single throw. He then passed one end of the rope through the loop on the opposite end and tugged until the rope was tightly secured around the rafter.

"The letter," Radan ordered. "Do not fail me."

"I will take it to every lord," Vid assured him. "They will know what Lord Nergal has done."

Satisfied, Radan slid the noose over his majestically elongated cranium and then tightened the rope around his neck. Vid stepped back. Radan suspected the brute watched him with admiration. He could not believe he would die smelling a stinky Gourman.

Radan recited that stupid proverb, "Neither fortunes nor flowers last forever."

He stepped off the desk. The snare tightened.

He choked, kicking his feet uncontrollably in the air. As tears blurred his sight, he saw Vid move in his peripheral vision, tossing something into the fire.

The letter!

All of a sudden, his servant stood at his feet collecting the severed hand from the desk. He wrapped it in the black linen once more. Vid then looked up at Radan and smiled. "Not so smart after all."

Joshua Robertson

Taste of Freedom

Grape juice spilt on white carpet
and smeared across pouty lips
of a silky maid. Bra snapping,
freeing the bosom from their

virgin alps. Cry in descent
when seeing the seed planter
who forsook and mistook love
with a broken branch. The path

among the tranquil greenery
with painted daisies. The man
standing boldly with pants dropped
With rent drizzling at the knees.

Daddy, who is not father,
returns from no windows and
decorated metal teeth, clenched
tight as her fists of freedom.

When the liquid splatters on
pretty rich threads walked upon
daily by the maid. The man
unhinges a bra no more.

Taste of Freedom was written as freestyle poetry, so if it holds to a particular form, I am unaware of it. It was a test of using figurative imagery in describing a sexual assault victim exacting justice when their abuser returns. This was written in response to a personal story that was shared with me in private, and I wanted to write an alternate outcome to the situation that would alleviate the traumatic impact it would otherwise impose on my psychological well-being.

Joshua Robertson

The Devil and the Romani

(originally translated by Albert Henry Wratislaw)

An old Romani woman had come down on her luck and needed money and could think of nothing else to do except submit herself as a servant to the devil. She went to where the devil lived and asked for work to earn enough coin to retire and live carefree into old age.

The devil, ornery as he was, knew the Romani woman would die before she earned enough to leave his service.

Still, he handed a pail to the Romani and said, "I will give you what you wish if you bring me firewood and water regularly and put a fire beneath the kettle. Go yonder to the well and draw some water."

The Romani went off, got some water in the pail, and drew it up with a hook. But being old, she couldn't draw it completely out and was obliged to pour the water from the pail in order not to lose it in the well. She knew she could not return to the devil without a full pail. She then took some stakes from a wooden fence and used them to grub around the base of the well, as though she were digging.

In the meantime, the devil waited and waited, but the Romani did not return with the water. After a while, the devil went to meet her and without thinking inquired, "Why do you loiter so? Why haven't you brought the water you were sent to fetch?"

"Loiter? Never would I! I want to dig out the whole well and bring it to you, so you would never have a need to fetch water again when I have gone."

"You have wasted time. Because you have not brought the pail in time, the firewood I have has diminished." In frustration, the devil drew out the water and carried it home himself.

The old Romani sighed, "Eh! If only I had known the firewood was already burning, I should have brought it long ago."

When they returned to where the devil lived, he said, "Go yonder to the forest and bring wood for the fire."

The old Romani woman started off, but rain assailed her in the forest and wetted her through and through. The old woman caught a cold and could not stoop down after the sticks. She knew she could not return to the devil without an armful of wood. She then pulled bast in heaps, connecting the strips together, and then went round the trees tying one to another.

The devil waited and waited until he was out of his wits on account of the Romani. After a while, the devil went to meet her and saw what was going on. "What are you doing, loiterer?"

"Loiterer? No such thing am I! I want to bring you wood and so I'm tying the whole forest into one bundle. I would hate for you to ever need to fetch wood again when I have gone."

With a snort, the devil took up the firewood and carried it home himself.

By and by, the devil went to an older devil to ask for advice, saying, "I have hired a Romani, but she is terribly daft, and I end up doing the work I ask of her."

"She leads you by the nose," said the older devil. "When she lies down to sleep, you should kill her and let her trouble you no more."

In agreement, the devil went home that night with the intent to murder her, but the old woman noticed something was off. When they lay down to sleep, the old woman put his fur coat on a bench where he usually slept and then crept into a corner. The time came and the devil thought she was in a dead sleep. He took his iron cub and beat the fur coat until he was sure that the Romani was dead.

A moment later, when the devil was back in his own bed, he heard a grunt.

"What ails you?" asked the devil.

"Oh, a flea bit me."

The next day, the devil went again to the older one for advice. "I cannot kill her," said the devil, "for when I smash her with all my might, she only says a flea bit me."

"Then pay her up now," said the elder devil, "as much as she wants. And let her trouble you no more."

The old woman chose a bag full of gold coins and went off at the devil's command. The devil eventually became sad about the money lost and consulted the older devil again.

"I am much too poor for the old Romani asked too much. Whatever should I do?"

"Overtake her," said the elder devil, "and say that whoever kicks a stone the best so the sound travels three miles shall have the money."

The devil did just that, catching up with the old woman and saying, "Stay, Romani! I've something to say to you. Let us kick a stone, and whoever kicks the loudest will take the gold coins."

"If that is what you wish, son of the enemy. Now then, kick away," said the Romani.

The devil kicked again and again until the clang resounded in their ears.

She then took out her waterskin and poured water on the stone.

"Eh! What is that you are doing, you fool?" the devil cried.

"If the stone is too dry when I kick it, water will flood this whole area and drown us both and I am afraid I don't know how wet it should be."

The devil was afraid of drowning and said, "Let us not risk it. You can keep the gold coins for now."

The devil returned to the elder and said, "The Romani can flood the land by kicking a stone. Whatever should I do?"

"Overtake the old woman once more," said the elder devil, "and say that whoever throws a club the highest shall have the money."

The devil did just that, catching up with her again, and saying, "Stay, Romani! I've something to say to you. Let us toss a club, and whoever throws it the highest will take the gold coins."

"If that is what you wish, son of the enemy. Now then, throw away," said the Romani. "But be warned that I've two brothers in heaven, both smiths, and they will want these tools as hammers or tongs to create weapons to kill devils."

The devil threw his club, so it whizzed to the edge of the clouds and was scarcely visible.

When it landed on the ground, the old woman then took the club and held it up, shouting, "Hold out your hands there, brothers. I give you a gift to create weapons to kill devils"

The devil was afraid and said, "Ah, stop! It would be a pity to lose my club. You can keep the gold coins for now."

The elder devil advised him again. "Overtake the Romani once more and say that whoever runs fastest to a certain point shall have the money."

The devil did just that, catching up with her again, and saying, "Stay, Romani! I've something to say to you. Let us race and whoever is the fastest will take the gold coins."

"I am far too old to race you, son of the enemy, but if you can catch my young son, I will give you the money," said the Romani. It was then that she saw a hare in the firwood. "There he is! His name is Hare, and he is only three days old. Catch him up!"

The devil ran and ran, but the hare went hither and thither in bounds, leaving the devil in the dust.

"Bah!" The devil cried. "He doesn't run straight. You can keep the gold coins for now."

"In my family, no one ever did run straight. We run as we please."

The elder devil advised him again. "Overtake the old woman once more and say that whoever wrestles to prove their strength shall have the money."

The devil did just that, catching up with the gypsy again, and saying, "Stay, Romani! I've something to say to you. Let us wrestle and whoever is the strongest will take the gold coins."

"I have been traveling for some time and thus far too tired to wrestle you, son of the enemy, but you can wrestle my father. If you win, I will give you the money," said the Romani. She led the devil to a hollow rock where a bear did reside. "My father is so old that for the last seven years, I have had to carry his food into his cave. Go in there and wrestle him if you think yourself stronger."

The devil went in and said, "Get up, long-beard! Let us have a wrestle."

In a short time, the bear did hug the devil, clawed him up, and threw him down on the floor of the cave.

The devil ran from the cave in fear. "He is far too strong. You can keep the gold coins for now."

One last time, the elder devil advised him. "Overtake the Romani and say that whoever whistles best, so it can be heard for three miles, shall have the money.

The devil did just that, catching up the gypsy again, and saying, "Stay, Romani! I've something to say to you. Let us whistle and whoever is the best will take the gold coins."

At once, the devil whistled so it resounded for three miles to prove his skill.

"Do you know when I whistle, you will go blind and deaf?" the old woman asked. "It will be best if you bind up your eyes and ears to be safe."

He immediately wrapped his eyes and ears in thick cloth. Once bound, the old Romani took a mallet for splitting logs and banged it twice against the devil's ears.

"Oh stop! Oh, don't whistle again or you'll kill me! May ill luck smite you with your money! Go where you will and never be heard of again!"

And the old Romani took her coins and retired, living carefree into old age.

Joshua Robertson

His Name

I'd hear it whispered, in burdened disdain,
My flesh burns with fury, masking this pain,
You soothe nothing when you say his name.

Torment me, you do when we play this game,
I question whether your love is in vain,
I'd hear it whispered, in burdened disdain,

You force me to endure this hateful shame,
Demanding I stop and stay in my lane,
You soothe nothing when you say his name.

In your head, it is likely all the same,
Speak of him with nothing to lose or gain,
I'd hear it whispered, in burdened disdain,

Once again, it is ignorance you claim,
Unaware you simply deepen the stain,
You soothe nothing when you say his name.

In the end, I become the one to blame,
A battle lost, leaving me to be slain,
I'd hear it whispered, in burdened disdain,
You soothe nothing when you say his name.

His Name was me trying my hand at villanelle form, known for its rigid rhyme scheme. This poem was written after experiencing infidelity in a relationship and then attempting to heal the hurt and move forward. In the months following, while trying to mend the broken relationship, my partner continued to speak positively of the individual and maintain their connection despite my protest.

Joshua Robertson

Devourer of Maidens

The maiden curled her slender fingers in the leather cords that connected to the bridle of the stallion. She detested this animal as much as the thought of childbirth. The horse had no sense of duty, always scarpering off at the first sign of danger.

"They are no longer giving chase, Raisa. Slow down!" Her thighs tightened on either side of the saddle, holding fast to the fickle mount.

Realizing she was still holding the small container in her free hand, she released the vial to the blur of the landscape beneath her. She licked the last drops of green liquid from her lips as an afterthought of her decision.

"Just…just a bit further, Raisa," her voice cracked. She did her best to maintain her calm, finding slight hilarity that she was giving the stallion mixed signals. Noble or not, it was clear that the strength of her mind was already dwindling.

The maiden was uncertain of how she felt at this moment. She had cried as heavily as seawater spilling from a ship's scupper that morning, but it had ended after being chastised by her father, the King of Ardaim. He could not save the other maidens, nor could he protect her.

"Raisa…don't stop," she insisted again, as though reinforcing an endless lie. Her head was light as the stallion tore over another uneven hill toward the mouth of the dragon's cave.

Clawed feet tore into the soft soil of the spring earth as the serpent body of the dragon crashed in front of the woman upon the horse. The large horn-tipped wings unfurled like a lady's fan, red and gray as the loam found beneath the topsoil. There was no unearthly roar, no bellow of thunder from the beast. Still, Raisa halted mid-step and reared, throwing the woman from its back.

The woman cried out, reaching for the ill-bred animal. Her hands fell short of the mount as it coiled away from the massive dragon. Raisa whickered with its nostrils widening in horror, never taking a second look towards the collapsed rider. In an instant, the horse was fleeing back the way they had come, leaving the woman stranded in the wild country.

The dragon ignored the bolting stallion. It huffed heavily and swept its head sideways to leer at the fallen woman, "Certainly before, I have not had a maiden come to me. A pleasant surprise, this is!"

The woman's jaw quaked uncontrollably, her lungs burning. Pain seared through her joints as she tried to talk, but words could not be formed. She twisted and thrashed about on the ground like an infant learning to stand.

The deep brown slivers that made up the serpent's eyes widened, giving light to golden shimmers around the iris, "To whom do I owe the pleasure?"

The dragon was patient in waiting for her response. The beast was timeless, feared by all, and threatened by none. Let alone a hapless female flopping on the palpable floor.

She coughed harshly, wheezing uncontrollably. The maiden did her best to steady her breath, realizing she did not have any incentive to move from her supine position. Despite her best attempts, her voice was shaking as though she had no brains about her, "Krutina Duveck of Ardaim, daughter of King Dudin, Heir of Hjaltok, and Keeper of Flockadalr, the Ashen Claw of the West."

The dragon was obviously impressed, cooing through curled lips, "A princess maiden? A pleasant surprise, indeed! Noble blood always is honeyed, a thick crimson syrup without any matched taste! The perfumed scent is nearly as sweet as the delicate flowers of Floroand!"

She knew the beast intended to eat her but had not thought that it would take such delight in tearing through her flesh.

"Surely you know of me, Princess?"

Krutina lay still, her leg aching through her toes. "I know you, Lamia the Devourer!"

"If you know me then you know where I roam. Why have you come here? You surely know I enjoy the flavor of maidens."

"I know that," she faltered. She had not thought of any reason to give the dragon for her coming. Krutina asked the only thing that came to her mind, "Why must you eat us?"

"It is the way of things, Princess. Do you raise question when you feed upon the cattle or the sheep?"

"But you only consume women!"

"Do you not prefer the veal to the bull? It is only natural to have our preferred tastes."

"You have fed upon every girl of age within Ardaim for the past ten years. You have brought my people nothing but angst! When would you have your fill? You are nothing but a vile creature!"

"Boldly spoken!" Lamia tittered with amusement, flashing teeth stained with a thousand corpses. "I cannot say that any other of your kind has been so daring to speak to me in such a manner. It is heartening to know that some humans do have a backbone! The question is whether yours will withstand my bite?"

Lamia chortled all the louder.

"We will see."

Lamia snapped playfully towards Krutina, "Tell me, Princess. Does this mean that you are the last maiden of Ardaim?"

"I am the last," she hissed. "You will torment this Kingdom no more!"

"Indeed! Tell me what Kingdom lies adjacent to your own?"

"No!" she screamed, voice echoing over the hilltops.

The dragon silenced the princess, snatching the girl from the ground with its mouth, tearing through flesh and bone. As Lamia gnashed its teeth, absorbing the noblewoman, its stomach churned. The beast's head spun, and its vision blurred. With a grunt, Lamia collapsed to the ground in a heap. It heaved frantically attempting to empty its insides, but it was too late.

The poison that Princess Krutina had swallowed melded effortlessly into the bloodstream of the reddish-brown dragon. Before the sun lowered beyond the horizon, the gold lining surrounding the serpent's brown irises faded.

Lamia the Devourer breathed no more.

The Hungarian Whore

Trails of sin-stained, blood-soaked threads
lead to the lady's chamber.
Red drink upon crimson lips,
No droplets left to savor.
The bone basin overflows,
Her fabric has come undone.
Muffled cries, unspoken lies,
Deathlessly unheard by none.

The Hungarian Whore is written in syllabic verse and is a nod to one of the most intriguing women in history, Countess Ecsedi Báthory Erzsébet. She was a wealthy, powerful noblewoman from the Kingdom of Hungary in the late 16th and early 17th centuries. Legends suggest that she bathed in the blood of virgins to retain her youthful appearance. This short poem was meant to remind us how the legacy we leave behind after death may not always be welcomed.

Joshua Robertson

Ice Age

An
ice age
melts away.
A memory
from my history.
The endless blackness breaks,
to heaven's faith-filled flamelight,
The twilight giving way to dawn,
Thawing the frost from my frightful youth,
For a life of hope: fair and fine, forsooth!

Ice Age is an etheree I wrote sometime between adolescence and young adulthood. I was sitting in my vehicle, waiting for a college class to start, and considered the trauma I had experienced through my younger years. I wondered whether I truly had the liberty to craft a better life. I recall thinking about how I could either choose to remain frozen in my fear or grow from my experience.

Joshua Robertson

Jack Spratt

The butter-yellow bulb hung from the long-exposed wire in the center of the room. Jack took another swig from his rum bottle and stared at the buzzing light with a crooked smile. A giggle bubbled from his lips without warning, surprising him. He stifled a laugh and leaned back against the back of the rickety chair. The wood popped slightly, smashed between his thin frame and the ramshackled corner of his old home.

The sun had disappeared over the horizon an hour ago, lost beyond the single, broken window on the far wall. Supper was stewing, and he was starving.

His attention shifted to the red-stained floorboards beneath his feet, almost glowing in the pale room. He could not tell if the floor illuminated the light or the other way around. But the sight amused him. He shifted his weight again, sliding his elbow onto the wooden table next to him. He fingered the long handle of his trusty ax with his other hand and took another drink. He grinned wider, letting his mind wander, and muttered,

> *"Jack and Jill went up the hill,*
> *The damn thing was a blunder,*
> *Jack fell down,*
> *And broke his crown,*
> *And Jill is six feet under."*

"Shut your jabbering pie hole, Jack," Joan said with a heavy snort. His wife, an oversized woman with more fat than clothes, stood over the stove in the opposite corner. She meticulously stirred the creamy, black goop in the giant pot. "I am sick and tired of hearing about your dead fiancée. You are mine. Do you hear me? Mine."

Jack put the bottle back to his lips, feeling the spiced liquid slide down his throat. His fingers gripped the wooden handle of the ax as he drank.

Joan continued with her usual yammering. "That dew-dropper didn't have an ounce of brains in her. You should be lucky to have found a woman as fine as me."

He laughed, almost spitting out his rum. His wife did not seem to notice.

"Go on. Enjoy your giggle water. The stew is almost done, and the pie is nearly cooled." Joan leaned over the pot and sniffed the lingering stench.

Jack smacked his lips, catching sight of the meat pie set out in front of him. Steam roiled from the patterned topping. The dessert looked tasty. He said,

> *"What are little girls made of?*
> *Sugar and sweat,*
> *Makes Jack's hunger whet,*
> *That's what little girls are made of."*

"Yes, yes," Joan replied. "Nothing compares to a good, mincemeat pie. Now, keep that pussycat away."

He squinted at their black tabby yanking a clump of meat from the edge of the pie crust. Something shimmered on the end under the faint light, like a piece of jewelry. He swatted his hand at the animal, and the cat leapt off the table, taking its prize. He wondered out loud.

> *"Sing, sing, what shall I sing?*
> *The cat's run away with Pudding's ring."*

His wife swung her head around, her beady eyes staring coldly at him through puffy bags of skin. When she spoke, Jack gawked at her bleeding gums and missing teeth. The remaining few were as yellow as the light. "You best stop that pussycat from eating any more of that pie, or I swear I will beat you within an inch of your life, Jack Spratt. We did not go to all this trouble to feed the cat!"

Jack replied,

> *"Four and twenty young girls,*
> *Baked in a pie.*
> *Pease, Goldie, Little Red,*
> *They all did love to die."*

His wife responded with a sneer as she served their supper. Slopping together two platefuls of food, Joan waddled over to the table and slid a dish in front of Jack. The blackened goop oozed across his plate, beckoning to be devoured. He hovered forward intently to stare at the dark mass.

"The blood can color the stew but it makes the fat extra tender," Joan said, sitting in the chair across from the table. The woman scooped up a bite and sipped from her spoon. The remains of the Pease Pudding dripped off her lip. Joan hurriedly used a finger to slosh it back toward her tongue with a slobbery slurp.

Jack said,

> *"Pease Pudding hot, Pease Pudding cold,*
> *Pease Pudding in the pot, nine days old.*
> *Some like it hot, some like it cold,*
> *Some like it in the pot, nine days old."*

"Perfectly aged," Joan agreed with a grunt.

Jack took his first bite of the sludge and washed it down with another swig of his rum. If anything, the alcohol intensified the flavor. Glancing up at his wife, he saw her plate had already been emptied. Now, her fingers were in her mouth, rubbing the taste of the grunge from her gums. As if discovering a treasure, Joan plopped her finger nearly down her throat and sucked on it with enthusiasm. Her eyes momentarily darted toward his dish, as though his supper might jump over to her meal.

With a chuckle, he slid his plate over to his ever-hungry wife. She grabbed ahold of it with eager hands and devoured his still hot meal. He sang,

> *"Jack Spratt could eat no fat,*
> *His wife could eat no lean.*
> *And so betwixt the two of them,*
> *They licked the platter clean."*

Joan smiled before her face suddenly etched with concern. She dipped down in her chair. "Jack, I hear voices out by the mulberry bush. Go creep to the window and see who is out there."

He drank from his rum bottle and stared at his wife for a moment. He listened but heard nothing.

"Hurry, Jack," Joan barked between clenched uneven teeth. Her eyes seemed exceptionally beady tonight.

Jack snorted.

"Jack, be nimble.
Jack, be quick."

"You best be," Joan demanded. "Now, off with you before I beat you with my stirring spoon right upside your broken crown."

Jack slid off his chair and tiptoed across his reddened floor to the broken window across the room. The bulb swayed over him, crackling and humming louder with every step. Sneakily, he finally poked his head over the ledge of his windowpane and looked through the sharp ends of the fragmented glass.

The faint yellow light from the bulb flooded the frayed yard, stopping nearly half a foot from the hedge alongside his house. Through the twisted, dead branches of the mulberry bush, he could see two bodies, one plump and the other scrawny, shuffling back and forth.

"Miss Muffet. Miss Muffet." The gangly, long-legged one, who Jack recognized as Mr. Eencey Spider, hunkered down behind the brush. "Is this where Mr. Spratt lives? Are you certain?"

Stuffing a spoonful of something in between her eager lips, the woman known as Maggie Muffet chewed with the passion of Jack's wife.

"Miss Muffet?" Mr. Spider raised his hand as though he meant to poke her, but suddenly retracted his hand. "Pease Pudding will not have much time. We must be vigilant. Her life depends on it."

Jack raised himself up a bit more on his toes to see Maggie adjust her thin, wire-rimmed glasses and examined Mr. Spider. "Her life? Do not be dramatic," she clucked between her driveled smacking. "Mr. Spratt has never hurt anyone. He has been quite distraught since his fiancée's death."

Mr. Spider cleared his throat, standing awkwardly with his knees half-bent and his boney buttocks sticking out behind him. The threadlike man crossed his arms across his chest. "I have told you a hundred times that his sadistic, worm-infested wife is manipulating him. But do not be fooled. Mr. Spratt is a cold-blooded killer and worse. He is wanted in seventeen counties."

"Nonsense," Maggie said loudly, cheeks jiggling as she shook her head. "Mr. Spratt is a fine gentleman and was once an educator just like his predecessor, Mr. Crane. I cannot believe you have dragged me out here at this hour to spy on him."

"How can you believe such a dastardly thing? Look at the house! It is in shambles," argued Mr. Spider in hushed tones.

"If we suspected every person who had poor housing in Shadybrook was a deranged killer, then half the town would be jailed. For goodness sake, be sensible."

"Jack," Joan hissed from behind him, pulling him away from the outside conversation. "Who is it? What do they want?"

Jack gulped, turning to face his wife.

"Little Miss Muffet, sat on a tuffet,
Eating her cottage cheese,
Along came a Spider,
Who sat down beside her,
And said, 'Where the hell is Pease?'"

"Oh Lord," Joan moaned, scooting out of her chair and crossing her arms. "We have been found out by those dew-droppers, Jack. You need to take your ax and go end the two of them."

Jack could only stare blankly at Joan for several seconds. Finally, he gulped the rest of his rum from the bottle.

She flared her nostrils. "Why are you sitting there, you dupe. Go on out there and be quick about it," Joan demanded, pointing to the door.

Jack sighed with defeat and made his way to the table with drooped shoulders. Scooping up his trusty ax, he slid out of the home.

With the door shut behind him, Jack twisted back to face the cracked blue wood. He examined the number 14 hanging crooked above the knocker and thought of Jill. She would never ask him to do something as dastardly as kill, but then again, she was dead. Jack wanted to refuse Joan, but he could think of nothing clever to say.

And so, he crept toward the mulberry bush. Quickly, he found Miss Muffet and Mr. Spider still speaking heatedly with one another.

Maggie Muffet crinked her neck and looked at Mr. Spider with a half-smile on her face, as though she understood what was going on. "You have brought me out here for a bit of a tussling, didn't you? That is what this is about, isn't it?"

"What?" Mr. Spider stepped back, scowling, nearly tripping over his floppy feet.

Jack ducked down behind the hedge, squinting at them in the dark.

"Oh, don't be coy, Mr. Spider. I saw the way you just tried to touch me a bit ago; and now, you are having to restrain yourself," said Miss Muffet. She gave a slow wink. "You are the only *bad* guy out here tonight."

"Stop. You are being ridiculous!" Mr. Spider growled under his breath, throwing his arms down to his sides awkwardly. He balled up his fists. "I have no interest in doing any tussling with anyone, especially you, Miss Muffet."

"You have been making eyes at me since I became your partner," she contended.

His face reddened. "I have not."

Maggie batted her lashes. "Oh…I thought you had. Are you certain?"

"Quite certain," he stammered.

With a frown, she hung her head, turning back to her bowl. She fiddled with the spoon and pouted. "I should be home enjoying my second supper."

Mr. Spider glared. "I allowed you to bring your creamy goop with you, did I not?"

Jack shuffled his feet, gripping his ax. He did not want to have to fight them both off at the same time.

Maggie wrinkled her nose. "My meal tastes better in the comfort of my own home. Besides, you did not even give me time to get properly dressed. I look like a bum out here hiding behind the shrubbery."

Mr. Spider cleared his throat, his face twisting with disgust. "Back to the matter at hand—"

"What, Mr. Spratt?" Maggie scoffed. "I told you Mr. Spratt is a fine gentleman. Let's go home and leave him alone."

Jack smiled. Maybe he could let them live.

"Pease Pudding has been missing for nine days."

She snorted with laughter. "And you seriously think she is inside?"

He spoke slowly as though he were choosing his words carefully. Jack almost heard the sarcasm. "I suppose you best prove me wrong. Why don't you wish Mr. Spratt a pleasant evening, and we will be on our way?"

Maggie responded, "I will if it means we can finally go back home and drop this case. You have been after this poor man for almost a week now."

Mr. Spider opened his mouth to talk but quickly snapped it shut.

"Don't give me any of this nonsense about girls missing as soon as Mr. Spratt married Joan," Maggie muttered, waddling past him to circle around the hedge. "Little Red. Goldie. Pease. They probably all ran away together but being snatched away by former teachers...." Maggie shook her head. "We don't need that type of negativity in Shadybrook."

"Of course not," Mr. Spider cooed behind her.

With a huff, Miss Muffet made her way across the uneven lawn. Jack snuck out of sight behind the mulberry bush. Maggie did not so much as look in his direction. She headed toward the uneven steps of his front door. Jack was going to have to act fast before she went inside to speak with Joan.

He gripped the ax firmly and stepped up to face Mr. Spider.

"Here we go 'round the mulberry bush,
So early in the evening."

"Mr...Spratt," Mr. Spider said with surprise, eyeing the weapon in his hands, "why don't you put down the ax?" The lanky, small-town cop took a step back, holding his hands up with the intent to defend himself.

Jack smiled and for a second to make sure Miss Muffet was out of sight. He did not see her anywhere in the yard.

A moment later, he heard a knock and his wife bellowed. "Who is it?"

His wide grin quickly vanished when he turned back to Mr. Spider. The officer had pulled a gun from somewhere on his body and pointed it at Jack.

"Put down the ax, Jack," Mr. Spider said. "Your game is over. You are going to show me where the girls are and then we are going to take a drive to the station."

Jack, feeling the full effects of the rum he had been drinking, laughed out loud. Then, with a quick bounce, he spun on his heel and ran around the hedge.

Mr. Spider growled, lifting his gun to aim at Jack's retreating form before choosing to give chase instead. Round and round they went in circles around the brown-tipped bush, first one way and then the other. Jack giggled with glee, holding his ax to his chest all the while.

"All around the mulberry bush,
The Spider chased the bastard,
The bastard thought 'twas all in fun,
Oh! Jack is plastered!"

"Stop this Mr. Spratt. At once!" Mr. Spider shouted as they made another turn around the shrub. Jack only chortled louder.

Finally, as Jack circled between the bush and the house, Mr. Spider desperately sprang through the middle of the hedge.

"Jack, be nimble.
Jack, be quick."

Jack jumped sideways as Mr. Spider became tangled and tripped on the twisted branches. The lanky, scrawny butt of a man flew forward over fifteen paces and slammed into the side of the house. His gun flew from his hands and he groaned in pain.

Carefully approaching the man, Jack saw the metal spigot sticking out from his home. Blood oozed from Mr. Spider's head where he had struck the metallic object.

"Eencey Weencey Spider,
Fell by the waterspout,
Down came the ax,
And knocked poor Eencey out."

Before he could make any audible protest, Jack spun the ax, so the blade was turned away safely, and swung the base against Mr. Spider's skull. The cop slumped unconscious.

Inside, he could hear Joan talking through the window. "Aren't you a chubby one? Yes, fatter than the children. Much fatter."

"Excuse me?" He heard Miss Muffet stutter.

Jack ran for the front door. He barely saw the 14 on the front before he burst through.

Miss Muffet bounded backward at his sudden entrance, eyeing him suspiciously. She had one hand on her stomach and the other over her nose. "Mr. Spratt, where is Pease Pudding?"

Jack dipped his head toward the large pot on the stove.

"Pease Pudding hot, Pease Pudding cold,
Pease Pudding in the pot, nine days old.
Some like it hot, some like it cold,
Some like it in the pot, nine days old."

Miss Muffet dropped her jaw in revulsion. Joan swelled up her chest. "Do not pretend to be surprised. We eat children, Miss Muffet. You had to have known before coming. So, tell me, why are you really here? Did you want a taste?"

"Mr. Spider told me. I didn't—" Crumbling to her knees, Maggie gagged. Her own supper quickly painted the filthy floorboards in whitish chunks. She clung to the reddened planks in misery.

"Something the matter?" Joan chuckled. She leaned down until her nose almost touched Miss Muffet's hair.

Jack watched incredulously as tears forced themselves from the corners of Maggie's eyes as she fought from heaving over and over again. Her entire body convulsed with disgust.

Miss Muffet managed to choke out, "You won't get away with this."

"Too late," Joan murmured with a soft laugh. "We already have. And you will be the next to fill our pot. We could feast on you for weeks."

"No. No. No." She whimpered, weakly swinging for Joan with her palm. The effort was minimal, but Joan responded with full force. Knocking her hand away, she slapped Miss Muffet across the cheek.

Maggie fell into her puke, her face stinging from the strike. She cried out, nauseous.

Joan gleefully raised her voice. "Oh yes. Nothing like tenderizing the meat before putting it on the fire." The fat around her chin jiggled with joy. "Her legs look so tasty. Take off her leg, Jack."

Jack tapped his finger to his chin, eyeing Miss Muffet and then Joan. As if making up his mind, he lifted the wood ax in his left hand, slinging the blade upright.

Maggie shuffled back on the floor, adjusting her wire glasses. "Nooo! Please." Maggie cried out, trying to crawl away.

"I'm hungry, Jack," Joan shouted. "Take her leg off like a real man. Be something more than what you were to your dew-dropper of a fiancée."

With a giant step, Jack changed his target and flung the ax downward into his wife's thigh. Joan bawled, flailing backward with the blade ripping through her flesh. Her skin and muscle fell away from the bone.

"Jaaack!"

She crumbled into the wall, jerking, in a desperate attempt to wriggle away. The blade had only cut halfway through her thick leg. Tears bubbled from the corners of her beady eyes. "What…are you doing?"

He lifted the ax to swing again at the woman who continued to terrorize the memory of his beloved Jill.

She choked on her spit, pulling herself along on the floor. Her eyes caught sight of her blood pooling across the already stained baseboards.

With two strong bounds, Joan hurled her body through the already broken window. And abruptly stopped, suspended in air, her plump body wedged in between the square frame. She squealed and writhed against the broken glass as it pierced her rolls of fat.

Jack rushed to the back of his wife, hacking the ax down like he was chopping through wood. Over and over, he sliced and slashed. Until Joan's screams stopped and her body was bloodied and unmoving.

He let go of the handle and found his way back to his chair in the corner. Covered in her own vomit and trembling in fear, Miss Maggie Muffet watched as he casually reached for the pie.

Jack plucked out a small, chubby piece of meat and flung it into his mouth.

"Little Jack Spratt,
In a corner sat,
Eating a mincemeat pie.
He chewed on a thumb,
And drank on his rum,
And said, 'Who will be next to die?'"

Joshua Robertson

Misplaced Fate

Never have I been a man to confess,
All options laid and made before my heart,
Why should I finish what I didn't start?
For a sad sack I am; no more, no less.

Yet here are two roads and what shall I lose?
Whether a king of slander or candor,
It matters not which route I meander,
For existence is nothing but a ruse.

Still, this twitting voice speaks to me in rhyme,
"Are you in accord or will you refuse?"
Prodding me to add meaning to life.

Life's a clock til it clangs its final chime,
Then death comes and whatever will we choose?
Live well or end it all with a dull knife?

Misplaced Fate is an Italian Sonnet that was attempted in a bout of madness while questioning themes of destiny and purpose. I wrote this almost two decades ago when mine seemed without direction and I wondered whether I was leading life, or it was leading me. These days, I typically side with the idea that free will is an illusion but that it is real enough to give our lives meaning, much like a simple story providing inspiration and can invoke emotions otherwise unknown.

Joshua Robertson

Inspiration Lost

Words once alive lay to rest on their deathbed,
My thoughts void now, immersed in woeful plight,
I struggle to think of what could be said,
When my pen droops over the paper white.

No sound leaps forth from this slippery tongue.
Somehow this midnight hour has silenced me,
To wake and wish, to sing what should be sung,
My muse eluding me despite my plea.

Go spit, brain! You woke me if you recall,
Opened my eyes to stare at a blank sheet,
To speak against my heart, my love withal,
To lack in feeling, do I dare entreat?

Give to me no more dreams; I shan't hear it,
Lest madness might overwhelm my spirit.

Inspiration Lost is an English Sonnet that was written after waking from unsettling nightmares with themes of love lost. I desperately wanted to capture the sense of loss and pain, detailing the horrors witnessed only moments before in the world of dreams. Yet I could not find the words. As I tried to recall the dream, it faded, and I was left with useless fragmented thoughts and a dwindling to write anything at all.

Joshua Robertson

God's Cock

The earth was barren; it was naught more than a wasteland of stone. God was saddened, knowing it was his responsibility to impregnate the land. Therefore, he sent his cock to make the earth fruitful without toil as only his cock had the power to do.

The cock descended into a black hole of a cave, deep in the rock, and sought a hidden fertile egg of wondrous power and purpose. The egg chipped against the might of the cock, and seven rivers trickled out of it. The rivers flowed to the settlement of humankind and soon all was green. Flowers and fruits sprouted over the land without the labor of its people. Wheat crops pervaded the soil, and the trees brought apples and figs, and when the cock came daily, a load of the whitest and sweetest bread would bud from the branches of a single Tree of Nurturance.

In this paradise, the people lived without care and only worked for amusement and merriment for nothing was needed. The settlement was protected from devilish storms by lofty mountains. It was here that no violence or fear could be found. Men were their own masters without worry of destroying themselves from ignorance, for everything was provided.

Each day, God's cock would come and hover high in the sky. It would stand erect and call for attention, wanting all eyes upon it. The cock would tell the people when to get up, when to take their meals, always what to do, and when to do it. The settlement was happy, and it was only God's cock that annoyed them with his continual crowing.

Before long, the people began to talk amongst themselves, and then they asked God to save them from the restless creature. "Let us fend for ourselves. We want to decide when we will eat, work, and rise for the day."

God hearkened to them. And so, the cock descended from the sky, crowing to them only once more. "Woe is me! Beware the lake!"

The people rejoiced and believed it had never been better with the cock no longer interfering with their freedom. The men and women ate, worked, and rose, all in the best order, as the cock had taught them. Yet, by and by, the people began to think they should not follow the cock's ancient crowing so obediently and began to live by their own order of things. In time, this led to illness and suffering; the people looked to the sky for guidance for they had forgotten the old ways, but God's cock was gone forever.

The cock's last words hung to memory, though the people knew not their meaning. A warning to dread the lake but no reason as to why; moreover, they had no lake in their valley. Only did they have the seven rivers that had spurted from the egg. The people suspected that a dangerous lake sat somewhere beyond the encircling mountains, yet any man who traversed to the top never espied the lake.

The hubris of humankind grew, and they crafted tools and pleasantries beyond what they had under the guidance of God's cock. The women made brooms from the wheat-ears and the men made straw mattresses, and no more did they go to the Tree of Nurturance for bread. Instead, they set it on fire and claimed they could make their own without any help from God, believing it would be finer than any bread that could be plucked from the branches. And so, the Tree of Nurturance fell, and the people gathered what bread remained, eating their fill, and then lay down by the rivers.

It was then, one man called Kowin spoke blasphemy, saying, "The seven rivers are wondrous, but I'd like to know why the water is exactly so much, neither more nor less."

Another replied, "Twas the craze of the cock. We were foolish enough to hear its false warning of a lake, which never was and never will be, but the cock ordered the waters to flow as so without tampering, too. I think it would be better to have more water."

At first, Kowin thought they already had water in abundance and any more might be too much, but the eagerness of his fellow man convinced him. "The sensible thing to do would be to break the egg up and drive as much water into each man's land, and we shall build dams so each might decide how much water is needed for themselves."

An outcry then arose across the valley and all the people rushed to the cave to break the egg to pieces. Kowin did not join them, but instead went to the top of the mountain to be the watchman for the lake beyond the mountain. The remaining people of the settlement ventured forth and stood around the egg. Together, they picked up stones and banged them against the shell. It split with a clap of thunder and so much water burst out that the people could not flee swiftly enough to avoid their deaths.

The paradise was filled with water and became one great lake. The flood reached the highest of the mountains, drowning all those who were too foolish to hear the warning of God's crowing cock. And so, Kowin was the only survivor from the destruction of mankind.

Kowin sat on the tallest mountain as the water continued to rise and he looked across the valley as pines and shrubs were covered, homes and people were submerged, and all the things humankind had crafted were lost.

Soon, he stood on a final rock with a single vine that was still dry. To the vine, he fled, and seized hold of it, worrying it could not save him due to being so thin and weak. Nevertheless, he commanded the vine to rescue him from the rising waters. The vine was agreeable to Kowin's demands and grew thick, and strong, and grew higher than the clouds. Kowin climbed the vine and nourished himself on the grapes and wine it produced for nine years until the flood ceased.

When the world became dry again, he descended, and thanked the vine, promising to always love wine above all things.

It was then that God came down from the heavens to see that Kowin had survived the flood which had emitted from the burst egg. He was so gigantic that Kowin could have danced up and down his nostrils and not been noticed, and still God came to him and said, "You have survived and will be called deathless, but you, too, have shown that you cannot be trusted and shall bow to me for all time, worshiping me for saving you from the flood your kind caused."

Kowin replied, "It was not you who saved me, but this vine from the earth and its gift of grapes and wine."

"I placed this vine for you to grab a hold of and save yourself from the waters," said God.

"Yet without my command, the vine would have been engulfed in the waters and I along with it, like the pines and shrubs in the valley," Kowin contended.

"Come," God said, "let us see which is the stronger. Whether it is I or you that should rule this earth. Yonder is a broad sea; the one that springs across it best shall have all that exists on its surface."

Kowin agreed.

And then God took off his coat and jumped across the sea, so only a single foot was wetted when he sprang to the dry land. He jeered at Kowin, who held his tongue. Instead, he drank wine and didn't get out of temper. Looking across the land, he saw the trees; without removing his coat, he cut one down and built a canoe. He then sailed across the sea for nine days and came on to dry land without even wetting a foot.

"I'm the stronger," said Kowin. "See how my foot is dry and yours is wet."

"You have overcome me," answered God. "You shall have the plains, the mountains, the sea, and the land beyond. But that is not all the earth, for also there is what is above us and beneath us. Come, then, let us see a second time which is the stronger."

God stood on a hollow rock and stamped on it with his foot, and it burst with a noise like thunder, and split in pieces. Beneath it a cavern broke open and gave light to three-headed dragons brooding. God battled the dragons, and one nicked his arm, drawing blood, yet he emerged from the battle victorious. He jeered at Kowin once more.

Kowin remained calm and drank his wine. Then, crafting himself a pickax, he found a hollow rock at the base of a volcano and broke it up over nine days. Again, the three-headed dragons were found in a cavern, but before they could assail him, liquid fire flowed like a broad river upon them. The dragons were slain without causing harm to Kowin.

"Again, you have bested me," said God, "but I do not acknowledge you as ruler of this earth until you overpower me in a third fierce contest. Yonder is a lofty mountain you have not before seen. It rises above the clouds, reaching my celestial table, where my cock sits and watches over my provisions. Now, take an arrow and shoot, and so will I. Whoever shoots the highest is the stronger, and then the earth will be theirs to rule, and all that is above and beneath it."

God shot his arrow, and it did not fall for eight days, and again he jeered at Kowin.

Kowin drank his wine and thought, and then crafted a long bow unlike any bow ever crafted. He then shot his arrow, and it did not come back for nine days, and then it fell. With it fell God's celestial cock for the arrow had pierced its wrinkled skin.

Kowin spat on it, knowing the cock would crow no more.

"It is done, and you are now the ruler," God said, "for you have prevailed in using your craft to show more strength than I might muster. You are a hero and no longer a man; you are a god of gods."

"I will now go and create my own lands among the thrice nine," Kowin claimed, "for it took me nine days to sail across the waters, nine days to crack the stone, and my arrow did fly for nine days as well. Beware of me for I will bring gifts that I devise entirely by myself and without the aid of any deity."

And off went Kowin the Deathless to enjoy his imperial dignity.

Joshua Robertson

Skalds of the West Sea

Whistled from singing skalds of the west sea,
a song of secret dreams dreamt by old men.
No better music played or sung could be
whistled from singing skalds of the west sea.
Harken to the hidden verse and be free,
Listen to the lyre play, and a tune when
whistled from singing skalds of the west sea,
a song of secret dreams dreamt by old men.

Skalds of the West Sea is triolet and may be one of the most enjoyable types of poems to write. This poem was written with respect to one of my favorite writers, J.R.R. Tolkien. In this poem, I am speaking of the wisdom of the Men from the West, the Númenoreans, now called Dúnedain, and how their longer life gave them wisdom that should be heeded by all mortals. While we may not have access to fictional men, the elders in our own world have plenty of wisdom to bestow upon us.

Joshua Robertson

About the Author

Joshua Robertson is an award-winning author, entrepreneur, influencer, and life coach. He has worked with children and families for twenty years in a variety of unique venues: a residential behavior school, a psychiatric treatment facility, and the child welfare system. He has functioned as a supervisor, an educator, a behavior specialist, and a therapist during his career. Known most for his Thrice Nine Legends Saga, Robertson enjoys an ever-expanding and extremely loyal following of readers. He counts R.A. Salvatore and J.R.R. Tolkien among his literary influences. He currently lives in North Carolina with his better half and his horde of goblins.

Read More from Joshua Robertson
www.robertsonwrites.com

Joshua Robertson

Other Fantasy From Three Furies Press:

threefuriespress.com

Out of the London Mist
Lyssa Medana

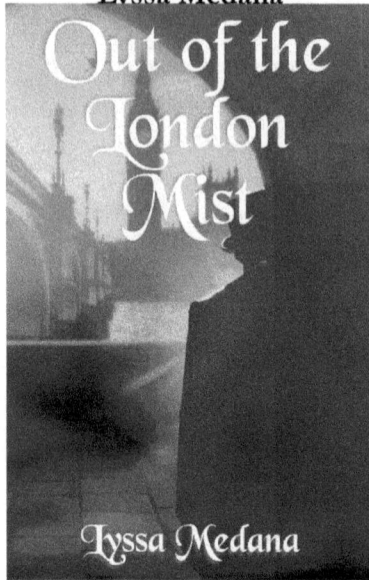

When news of his brother's murder reached him, aether pilot John Farnley raced back to his old family home.

While he comforts his bereaved sister-in-law, and tries to sort the family business and holdings, he also wonders why his brother, Lord Nicholas Farnley, had ventured into the cramped streets of the East End of London where he had met his violent end. The slums are a deadly place where life was cheap and murderous thugs preyed on the weak and lost.

Now, in the midst of a thick, London fog, something even more monstrous is waiting in the mist-shrouded shadows. Something that has been brought to life by the refugees crowding Bethnal Green and Mile End. Something his brother might have had a hand in creating.

Aided by his friend, the resourceful Miss Sylvia Armley, his own understanding of the aether lines that flow above London, and guided by the erudite advice of Professor Entwistle, John is forced to find his way through the darkest part of London to avenge his brother and stop whatever aether powered monster is lurking there.

Moss and Clay
Rebekah Jonesy

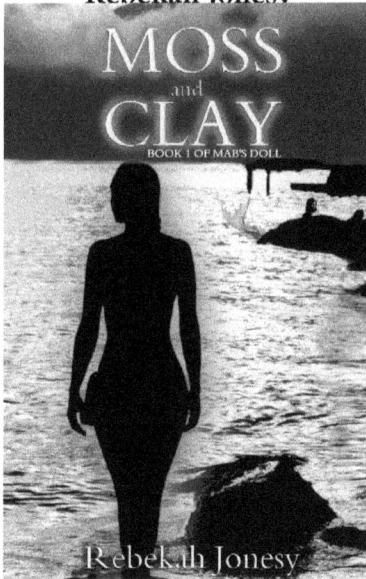

Moss, Clay, and Blood

A doll, crafted and given a mission by Danu, is brought to life by human and fae blood. Blood daughter of Mab, Queen of the Fae, Gillian must track down the fae in the Americas and bring them back under Fae Law. No one knows what is holding them there, or why no other rescue mission has returned. Not even the gods that sent them. Gillian must return the fae to the Underhill, or send them back to Danu.

Ren the Red Falcon
Joshua Robertson

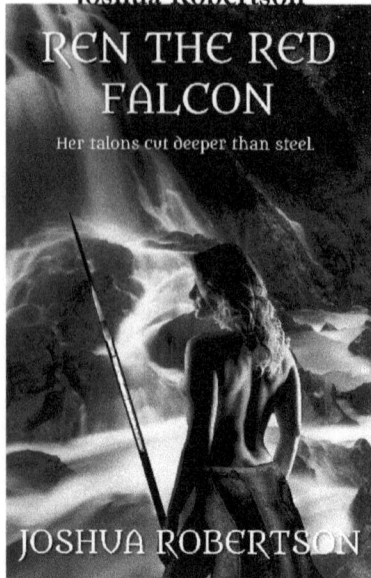

Taken by Aggath slavers as a child, Ren's youthful rage was tempered by the crack of a whip.

Season after season, she endured the wrath of those who slaughtered her kin and stole her life. Years later, when her captors are unexpectedly defeated by a company of savage barbarians, Ren briefly tastes freedom before being ensnared once more to be gifted to another tribe as a token of peace. Now, with thralldom threatening her future once more, she must learn to rekindle her inner fire or forever suffer a life of servitude.

The Suffering
Robert Cano

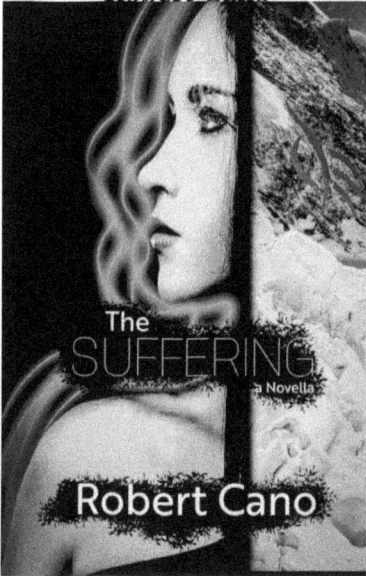

After twelve long years of ongoing warfare between the Fae and the Satyrs in her kingdom, Devani is finally heading home. The war was on the doorstep of her father's land when she was sent to stay in Yor'lon, where the king and queen were supposed to treat her kindly. The war has shifted now, and it is time to go home.

But the princess soon finds herself in a position she never expected, especially so close to returning. Struggling against death itself, her will to survive is overwhelming. She finds a way to freedom and relative safety, but at what cost and for how long? It seems the gods have other plans for Devani.

The Dark Archer
Robert Cano

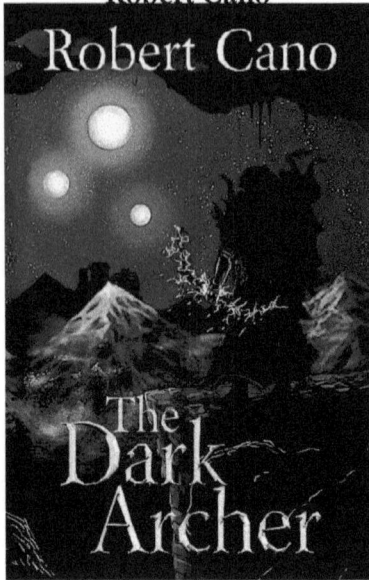

All he wanted was the safety of his princess. What he received was eternal torment. Bereft of a soul, a wraith who should have no ties to humanity, Bene wants nothing more than release from his twisted existence. Trapped between life and nothingness, he hopes to reclaim his soul and find the death he so desperately desires. Bene finds rare solace in the company of Feorin, a satyr war hero who chose exile over continuing the centuries long war with the Fae. He doesn't look at Bene with fear or contempt, but rather hope. If a wraith can find a path to redemption, perhaps he could as well…

Spade
S.L. Byrum

Pain.

How easily we address it in others, yet so often we deflect it in ourselves. At least. That's the case with the Plachette family, having just suffered a loss of a beloved wife and mother, Kathy.

Henry and his daughter must shoulder their grief and carry on, though chaos threatens to overtake them at any moment. As luck and legacy would have it, they are not alone in their struggle; a healing realm awaits them both on the tattered edges of the dream world and reality.

Spade, the conduit between the healing realm and human reality, has returned to warn, instruct, and to fight for them both, though her preference for the forest animals is hardly a secret. Henry and Drea must face their inner chaos in the dream realm to heal or succumb to an alluring fate of eternal emptiness. They are not alone in their battle, but the parallel between fantasy and reality will be questioned every step of the way.

The Sigil
Shakeil Kanish and Larissa Mandeville

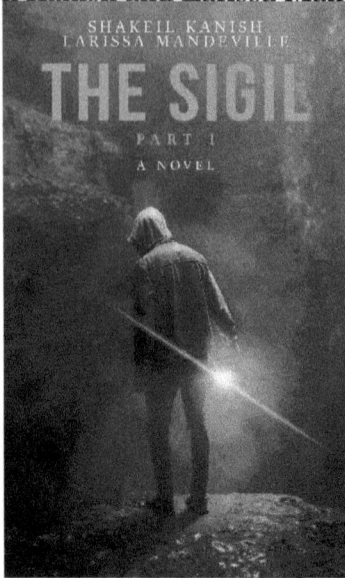

Lake's brother Devlin was murdered right in front of him. Simply because he was in the wrong place at the wrong time.

Why, then, does Lake think Devlin knew he was going to die before they ever set foot in the gas station that night? As he obsesses over his brother's death, Lake begins to uncover a hidden world full of forbidden magic and growing danger. Now he's stuck, caught between the world that his brother was meant for and his own. Lake is beginning to realize that no one and nowhere is safe.

Nova Rathers may not be especially powerful in the Mage world but she makes up for it with a magical bag of snacks and a body constructed by the Gods to slay. Desperate to be more than her lineage, she finds herself teamed up with a group of misfits and, in her mind, the weakest creature of all - a gida...a powerless human. Together, they start to unravel the lies that built their world and continue to hold it hostage. Nova's last year at Breyburn Academe was never going to be easy but she had no idea that it could ever get this bad.

Lake, Nova, and their newfound friends are about to find the truth behind what has been hunting them. But knowing is only half the battle. Even if they survive, will the rest of the world remain standing?

Mead and Mutton Pie

Joshua Robertson

Mead and Mutton Pie

Joshua Robertson

Joshua Robertson

Ingram Content Group UK Ltd.
Milton Keynes UK
UKHW011816170323
418736UK00001B/168